GEORGE PRINGATE'S LAST HURRAH

George Pringate's Last Hurrah

by

Stewart Hoffman

George Pringate's Last Hurrah

Copy editing provided by Good Tales Editing at https://goodtalesediting.com

Proofreading provided by the Hyper-Speller at https://www.wordrefiner.com

ISBN: 978-0-578-47265-2 (eBook)

ISBN: 978-0-578-47601-8 (paperback)

Library of Congress Control Number: 2019902691

1st published. March 26nd, 2019

Cover design by Stewart Hoffman

Contents

Chapter 1: America's Diner

Chapter 2: One Step

Chapter 3: Focus

Chapter 4: Be Brave

Chapter 5: The Finale

Acknowledgements

About the Author

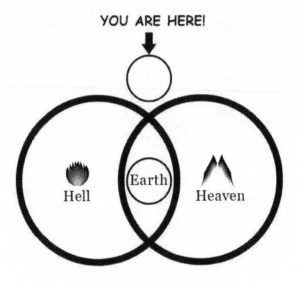

Chapter 1: America's Diner

I.

At first, all I see is daytime fog. Then I hear whispering, like a crowd settling down before a theater performance. As the voices fade, I hear an orchestra warming up, a mishmash of sounds as violins, cellos, and various brass and woodwind instruments yawn and stretch through scales. They abruptly stop as an unseen conductor taps a baton.

A door appears about a meter in front of me. A simple, metal frame double-glass door, all alone in the fog. The fog behind the door clears a little, and a plump woman carrying a coffee pot approaches and turns a sign around. Whatever this place is—and it does seem familiar somehow—it just opened for business.

I step through the door, and every sense is overwhelmed. The fog pulls back further to reveal a restaurant. A Denny's. My Denny's. America's Diner. My go-to place, just down the road from the Ford dealership where I take my car for its service. It's hard to tell what time it is as the white fog has only pulled back as far as the restaurant's windows. It smells like the morning shift, however, as coffee, cinnamon, and bacon are the predominant odors in the room.

I start to gain a sense of time and space and self, but I draw a blank when I try to remember my name. There is only more fog, though it seems to be clearing and I can see shapes forming in the mist. I look down at my hands, but they're not mine; they're thicker, stronger, with nicely manicured nails. I'm also wearing an expensive-feeling shirt and blue jeans over a body that feels lighter and stronger. I feel good, healthy, and I think about locating a mirror. Is this a lucid dream?

Someone calls out, "Mr. Pringate."

That's it, that's my name, George Pringate. The fog pulls back and a lifetime of memories flash by, an incomeprehensible collage of cool cars and movie stars, mixed in with family, lovers, and work.

I turn toward the sound of my name. In the corner booth, an attractive young woman waves and signals for me to join her. I have no idea who she is, but considering this is a dream, I'm encouraged by the direction it's taking. This woman is stunning. She has short black hair, rich sepia skin, and beautiful hazel eyes. She's also incredibly fit, wearing a shocking pink catsuit that advertises all her glorious curves. The ensemble puts in mind one of my favorite movies, *The Cannonball Run*, and the lovely Adrienne Barbeau sitting in that fantastic black Lamborghini Countach, tits on display, ready to seduce her way out of a speeding ticket. Her scenes with co-pilot Tara Buckman were always the most worn parts of the tape I had.

You don't usually find a woman like this having breakfast at Denny's.

She called me "Mr. Pringate" so we're probably not dating. Maybe this is going to be a more formal sexual fantasy, though we really should be some place nice like a wine bar or something if we're going to do this properly. I walk over to her as she slides herself free of the booth to stand and shake my hand.

"Hello, I'm Taylor Miller, your Transition Consultant."

"George Pringate," I confirm. *Transition Consultant?* I wonder if "transition" is a euphemism in my wet-dream fantasy. The real me is probably about to wake up with a raging hard-on. It's weird though that my name hasn't changed. Wasn't it supposed to be a combination of the street you grew up on and the name of your first pet? Hey ladies, I'm Chrisden Willoughby! Wow, my porn star name sucks.

She gestures for me to take a seat and I do. She joins me and not three seconds later, the plump waitress, and her coffee pot, arrive at our table. Her tag tells me her name is Sherryl.

"Get you two something to drink?" Sherryl asks.

I respond first. "I'll take a regular coffee, Sherryl." She smiles as I use her name, and I realize I know Sherryl. She was my server for years until one day someone else was filling my coffee cup. I had heard she was in a car accident and died. We had never spoken to each other in all the times we played waitress and patron. Familiar strangers. I can't recall ever seeing her smile at me before today.

"Nothing for me, thank you," Taylor says.

Sherryl turns over a mug in front of me and fills it with coffee. "I'll be back for your order in just a sec." She treats me to another smile before marching off to check on the other customers in the restaurant.

Taylor clears a space on the table, and from the bench beside her, she produces a large, blue ring binder and opens it. I take a sip of my coffee and wonder when this dream is going to get around to the sex part.

"First of all. This isn't a dream, as such, and we're not going to have sex," says Taylor as though she'd said that exact line a million times before. She looks back down at her notes in the binder.

I'm surprised that I feel relieved. I may currently not look or feel like myself, but if I'm honest, I know I wouldn't have the first clue how to approach a woman looking the way

Taylor does. If anything were to happen, I'm sure I would disappoint.

The story of my life.

II.

My first sexual anything came at an embarrassing age. I was twenty-two years old.

I had just finished my first month working at the Singh's Silicon call center—we sold everything from motherboards to monitors—and decided to take some of my earnings to a new pizza place that had opened near my apartment. It was a short walk away, which freed me up to drink as much as I wanted. A sweet treat in Anaheim, California: walking-distance beer.

Since it was a family place, I claimed a stool at the bar as far away as possible from the chaos and noise. Waitresses in tight white T-shirts and short shorts—the owner's idea of a uniform—delivered food and dodged advances from drunk patrons. Unruly kids ran around and made a nuisance of themselves while their parents consumed pitchers of domestic beer to douse any feelings of responsibility.

Later in the evening, after most of the families had gone, I returned from my fifth visit to the bathroom to find a woman sitting on the stool next to mine. A fresh pint of my favorite pale ale was waiting for me.

I stopped to take in the scene and give my buzzed brain a little time to process the image in front of me. My first thought was that a couple had claimed my place at the bar, but with most of the bar real estate available it seemed odd that they would deliberately park themselves in my spot.

She turned and smiled in my direction. I looked over my shoulder to see if she was looking at someone else.

"No, you, silly," she said. She waved me over and patted my stool. I liked her voice. She sounded like a local, and something in her manner and appearance told me she had money. She was older, in her late forties maybe, wearing a form-fitting black dress that showed off her shoulders and the top of her epic cleavage. Her straight black hair reached the base of her neck and covered one eye. The eye I could see scanned me from my Doc Marten boots up to my Angels baseball cap. I suddenly felt very self-conscious, and I played with my collar as I edged toward the fresh pint waiting for me. I understood why some might call her a cougar as I honestly felt like prey. My choices were fight or flight, or free beer.

"The bartender said that was your favorite," she said, gesturing toward the drink in front of me. I didn't know how to respond, so I just nodded. I took a sip and forced a smile. I tried not to stare, but her perfume seemed to reach out like a hand and gently lift my head and point it at her chest. Her actual hand reached over and encouraged me to look higher. "I'm up here, sailor."

I was sure this was a setup. At any moment the host of some *Punk'd* type TV show would appear, pretending to be this woman's irate husband.

"So, you live around here?" she asked. I nodded. I realized I should probably say something. My mind was spinning through every possible response I could think of, but they all sounded dumb.

She leaned in and looked me directly in the eyes. "Do you come here often?"

I shook my head. I could tell she was getting irritated by my silence.

"It's new," I managed to say.

"My goodness, it speaks!"

Smiling, she reached toward me and ran her hand up my forearm. I could feel my heart rate increase. Why did this always happen to me? The moment a woman got too close, or even hinted at wanting to be close, I'd start to panic. Thoughts crashed on top of each other leaving me with nothing complete to say. All I'd have to offer were a collection of fragmented ideas, dismissed notions, and if I did manage to say something, it would always come out sounding idiotic.

She released my arm and grabbed her phone from the bar. I figured I'd blown whatever this was, but she only looked at the time.

"Look, handsome, I don't have a lot of time. Let's go someplace a little quieter."

She slid off her barstool and straightened her dress. I looked back at my half-finished drink and hesitated. Despite the whirlwind of thoughts running through my head, space was always set aside for essential booze considerations. I wasn't accustomed to leaving drinks unfinished.

"Don't worry. I have booze at the house. Whatever you want," she said, with a wink.

When I get stressed or confused like this, a little part of me wakes up and provides guidance. House? *We're going to a house?* She's got booze. *Fuck yes.* Oh jeez.

As she walked away, I noticed the back was even more impressive than the front. For a moment there was clarity, and I realized I had a clear choice. My half-drunk beer or this improbable liaison, which might, just might, lead to a popped cherry. *Finally!*

I followed her out into the parking lot, my head down and hands in my pockets. I focused on her ridiculously tall heels as they knocked and scraped against the concrete. I felt like a bratty teenager again, picked up after high school following another visit to the principal's office.

Fuck me. She drove a Porsche. I didn't know which nine-eleven exactly, but it looked new and fast even while parked. She got in, and the convertible top elegantly folded back and disappeared into a space behind the seats.

I opened the passenger door and fell onto the plush leather seat. It was so comfortable, yet bolstered, holding me in place. The Porsche was a huge step up from my Ford. I focused on geeky details, comparing like-for-like between my car's interior and the Porsche. My air vents were bigger, but the arrangement of this car's interior was better. I touched the materials on the lower parts of the door panel and center console, the bits you didn't usually pay attention to and found them reassuringly comparable to my compact sedan.

The reality of my current situation, however, returned and snapped me out of the ridiculous Porsche versus Ford comparison test. First, as another whiff of perfume attacked my nostrils, and second, when the car shot forward and exited the parking lot.

"Better put on your seat belt," she said. "I like to drive aggressively."

We headed up to Anaheim Hills, the houses getting larger and further apart the longer we rolled. Our drive ended at what looked like a villa. I wondered if I was going to survive the night. For all I knew this might be some bizarre, rich asshole ritual, and I was today's sacrificial poor person. Nobody knew I went to the bar and no one would miss me until Monday when I didn't show up for work. And even then, it might have been a couple of days or a week before my boss considered calling someone to check up on me. I had no friends and no parents to contact. I had some extended family, but no one close. I suddenly realized this made me a juicy target for any would-be serial killer.

My buzzed brain, confused by the villa visuals, the slick car, the intoxicating perfume, and my beautiful curvaceous driver, had a notion of what was going to happen—a sexual scenario I'd watched many times online to the detriment of my eyesight.

This was the scariest night of my life, and I considered running away.

Snap, snap . . .

III.

Snap, snap . . .

"Earth to Pringate. Hello, Pringate."

The snapping of Taylor's fingers pulls me out of my daydream. Except it doesn't feel like a regular daydream. This is a complete memory, an ultra-high-definition, surround sound with Smell-O-Vision memory. It's like hitchhiking inside my own mind, seeing and feeling, but with no control, it seems.

"What was that?" I ask.

"That was a test run. As you go through this process, you're going to revisit moments in your life." Taylor finds the page of information she was looking for. "Ah, there you are."

She reads aloud. "George Pringate. Age forty-five, call center employee for the, wow, last twenty-three years. Was married, little family to speak of, no close friends, no current partners, no children. Education, high school, a few college courses that you didn't complete. Hobbies include sitting on your ass watching movies and drinking beer. You also have a fondness for classic movie cars. Tell me, does my outfit remind you of something?"

"Yes. It looks like the outfit worn by Adrienne Barbeau in the movie *The Cannonball Run*."

"A favorite of yours?"

"Absolutely. It's a classic."

"Would you say you feel stimulated?"

Hell yes! But I don't tell Taylor that. Instead, I nod nonchalantly and shrug my shoulders. I try not to look at the zipper edging its way down the front of her outfit.

She unclips a pen attached to her binder and makes a note. As the ink hits the page, it glows an intense, electric light-blue before disappearing completely. "We can use that."

I sneak a glance at the page she's reading. It's mostly blank. She runs her finger down the page and then turns it over. She seems genuinely surprised to not find more information.

"Wow, there's not much here," she says.

"What?"

"Well, you're here so I knew I'd have some work to do, but I didn't realize how much of a challenge this was going to be."

"Challenge? I mean—I don't—here? What's going on?"

Taylor closes her binder, folds her arms, and leans forward. "What do you remember before you walked into this restaurant?"

It's an interesting question because as I try to answer, only a few very specific moments in my life are available. I can count them on one well-manicured hand; my name, where I worked, and the time the rich lady in Anaheim Hills seduced me. Beyond that, I feel everything else is in the background waiting to be selected like an old vinyl record in a jukebox.

"Hardly anything," I finally say.

"Interesting. Usually, in these cases, there's more cognitive attachment to the past. The subject has achieved enough for the mind to hold on to some semblance of self. Not so much in your case." *My case?* I am about to ask more questions when Taylor unfolds her arms and sits back against her seat. She raises her arms and rests them on the back of the booth. She looks outside into the white fog and takes a deep breath. My attention is drawn down to her impressive chest as her breasts force the zipper on her outfit to slide downward. I have the distinct feeling this is being done intentionally to distract me.

It is working.

IV.

Things at the villa escalated quickly. After the Porsche was parked, we went inside, and I was led straight to the bedroom. She told me she didn't want to know my name, and she wasn't about to share hers. I decided Mrs. Robinson was appropriate.

She said we were at a friend's house, but I didn't believe her. I was sure if I looked at any of the overturned picture frames, I'd see her arm in arm with some superrich, yet frail and old husband.

The bedroom was bigger than my apartment, with a California King four-poster bed in the center. The bottom half of the walls were covered with ornate wainscoting and the upper half, gold and green striped wallpaper. I felt like that guy at the end of *2001: A Space Odyssey*. My entire life seemed fixed in one select moment, surrounded by expensive shit. I started to shake. Like, really shake.

At first, it was just my hands, but then my arms, shoulders, legs, and torso joined in. This wasn't mild jitters either; this was like a full-blown panic attack working its way through my body. My heart bounced around like a pinball inside my ribcage, and every sweat gland in my body turned on like a sprinkler. The only time I could recall experiencing anything remotely like this was when I was about to have my wisdom teeth removed.

The shaking got worse when my mystery vixen slinked back into the room. It was weird to think that if I'd had to choose between this bedroom and the dentist chair, I'd have been handing Steve Martin the pliers and telling him to get on with it already.

"Don't be nervous," she said.

Nope. Not helping.

"This is going to be fun," she said.

Still not helping.

Stop shaking. I'm trying. *You're still shaking.* I know!

She turned around and backed up to me. Her butt rubbed against my jeans and my limp dick, which was cowering in the darkness. I pictured a frightened mole.

Why, oh why, wasn't I hard? I got erections all the time. Cute girl at work walked by, boing! A sex scene in a movie, boing! I woke up most nights to find Mr. Johnson already up and at 'em, so why now, when my moment came, I couldn't. I had one job.

"Unzip me," she said.

Okay, it's only a zipper, you can do this. Still twitching like I'd been hit with a fucking Taser, I reached up and fumbled with the pull tab. I managed to pull it down, exposing her flawless back and the next stage of this waking nightmare—the bra and the hooks that stood between me and her fantastic tits. She shimmied a little, and her dress fell to the ground.

There was still nothing going on in my pants. I didn't know if it was the beer or the adrenaline, probably both. But

I felt it was time for drastic measures. I reached around and grabbed a boob and held on. The shaking got worse, and now my seductress was involuntarily moving with me. I was glad I couldn't see the expression on her face; she must have been so disappointed and confused. Her glorious breast felt heavy in my hand, but I couldn't help but picture Jell-O wobbling on a plate. It was shaped like a boob, of course.

I reached forward with my other hand and grabbed the other breast. Still nothing, and now I had two Jell-O desserts wobbling on a plate in my head. Two magnificent, sexy as hell, boob-shaped desserts. I suspected the next time I actually saw Jell-O dessert, I'd get a boner and be reminded of the night John Thomas died.

She reached up and gently took my hands, and then turned around. She smiled.

Please don't.

She winked

Please don't.

She grabbed my belt buckle. "Let's see what we're dealing with down here."

Nope. Nope. *Nope.* Not happening!

I ran away.

V.

"And you never returned to that pizza place," Taylor notes.

"Huh? Wait, how did you?" I ask.

"We know a lot about you, Mr. Pringate. So, you ran away," she smiles.

"I was . . . nervous."

Sherryl walks up to the booth with her order book in hand. "What can I get you? We do a great veggie-scram, pancakes, Jell-O surprise."

I look up at Sherryl, and she places her pencil-holding hand under her right boob. She gives it a jiggle and winks at me. Taylor opens her binder and hides behind it. I don't know why she bothers as I can still hear her laughing.

"Har har. So, you're in on this too?" I ask Sherryl.

"We all are, Mr. Pringate," says Taylor. She places her binder back down onto the table.

"Wonderful. You still haven't told me what the hell is going on here," I say.

"I'll get you our chicken-fried steak," says Sherryl. "Your favorite. You'll need to keep your strength up today."

She walks toward the kitchen, and I turn back to face Taylor. It's time for some answers. "Okay, how about you tell me what's going on? And why I can't see anything outside?" I point at the white fog obscuring our view of the street.

Taylor pushes her binder forward and folds her arms. She looks me straight in the eyes. "Fine, you want to jump right in? Here goes. Mr. Pringate, you are dead. You died."

I take a moment to process what I just heard. I'm not surprised because this is just another weird element in a bizarre dream. I think she's full of it of course, but sure. I'm dead. Why not? Bring on the elephant parade.

"Huh-uh, sure, I'm dead," I say.

"Yup," she confirms.

"And the afterlife is a Denny's?"

"Yours is."

"What a load of crap! This is just a dream—a vivid one, I'll grant you that, but still a dream." I pinch myself hoping to wake up. It doesn't work, so I try slapping my face.

Taylor continues to look directly at me, as though waiting for me to get a clue.

"Look, Mr. Pringate. We don't have a lot of time for explanations, so I'll get right to it. You are dead, and according to our records, you haven't lived either."

Say what now?

Taylor reaches for her binder, and after a brief search, she opens the rings and hands me a piece of paper in a plastic sleeve. She taps her finger on the Venn diagram at the top of the page.

It's simple enough, two large circles overlapping each other. Where they overlap, is a photo of Earth. In the area to the left, there's a clipart icon that looks like a flame, and in the area on the right, another clipart icon that looks like angel wings. Above the Venn diagram, a separate, much smaller picture of Earth has the words "YOU ARE HERE!" written in a big friendly font next to it.

"What the hell is this?" I ask.

"This is how the universe currently works," says Taylor.

I look at the diagram again. "Currently works?"

"Yes, we say currently because the human race is constantly evolving and ideas about life, death, and the beyond change frequently. Currently, a lot of people believe if you're good, you go to Heaven, and if you're bad, you go to Hell. The connections between time, space, and thought, Mr. Pringate, are not vague concepts or open for debate. Everything is connected, and the universe is listening to anything developed enough to transmit."

That last part sounds like something out of a *Star Trek* episode, but the diagram in front of me seems clear enough. If Taylor is telling the truth about my being dead—and I don't think she is—then this Denny's is some kind of fucked-up version of the Pearly Gates. I float this theory.

"Sort of," she says. She points at the bigger photo of Earth. "This is where you were, where good, what you might call Heaven, and bad, what you'd probably call Hell, exist in the same space. This is where people are born, live, and die. It's a mixture of both good and bad. When people die, their time on Earth is reviewed and based on how they lived their lives, they are transferred to the mostly crappy place or the mostly good place."

Taylor continues, "The concept of Heaven and Hell is a product of evolution. Given a trendy set of labels by human beings. There are no toga parties in the clouds, and no fiery pits to fall into. When the human race was just a glint in the eye of the evolutionary stew, there was nothing beyond death. Nothing at all. An animal died, it was no more, and we were animals.

"Then, as we evolved, our frontal lobes started to develop, and before we knew it, we were planning to meet for brunches and creating bucket lists. Cats, ants, goldfish— they don't plan ahead as we do, they don't invent iPhones, and subsequently, when they die, they are gone. No good place, no bad place. Once we humans started to ponder the mysteries of the universe, we also started to wonder about what happens after we die. When that happened, the universe listened, and voila, we got ourselves an afterlife. Which is a relief, right? I mean, what's the point of living a full life on Earth, learning and growing, trying to better ourselves, only to have it come to a complete stop at the end? The universe thinks that's unfair. The human race has been killing each other over the details ever since."

"And this is only for humans?"

"For the most part. But other species are starting to be heard. We're not the only intelligent animals on the planet, you know. Dolphins, nearly all the whales, and even dogs now have the beginnings of an afterlife. Most of them work in pretty much the same way as ours, except for dogs. There currently isn't a Hell for dogs. All dogs go to their version of Heaven, apparently."

I give Taylor a look that basically translates to "horse-shit," and I hand her the plastic-covered paper. She doesn't take it. "Okay, so you're saying, there wasn't a God, or Heaven, until the human race evolved enough to conjure one up?"

Taylor looks genuinely surprised. "Yes, that's pretty much it, only no God, as such, just sentient energy that keeps an eye on everything. More 'the force' from *Star Wars* and less the vengeful, judgmental, bearded gentleman sitting on a cloud. Once we've finished with your evaluation, you'll understand. With so many people in separate religions around the planet, the details got a little confused, lots of conflicting transmissions, but generally, most people believed if you were a good person, you got rewarded, and if you were an asshole, you got punished. What usually isn't talked about is how we live our lives. The universe, it turns out, is very particular about sentient thinking creatures like ourselves making the most of their living time."

I point to the smaller circle with the "YOU ARE HERE!" text next to it. "And this?"

"That is going to take a little time to explain."

Taylor looks at the large clock above the breakfast counter, then back at her notes. She pushes the binder rings back together and moves a large section of paper over and out of the way. After a quick scan of another page, she says, "You weren't big on exercising, were you?"

VI.

I got married when I was forty-two years old.

My time spent confined by holy matrimony didn't last long because I was, and I quote, a "soulless, boring, lazy sonofabitch." Something like that anyway. That declaration was loudly delivered a little over two years after my wife Donna said, "I do" and I responded, "Absolutely!"

I tried, I really did, but she wanted more out of life, apparently. The page she was on had designs on being upwardly mobile. Donna, being thirty-five years old, wanted to do a little more world exploring before settling down with kids and a big, luxurious, five-bedroom single-family home in Anaheim Hills. I would bring home the bacon, give her credit cards to play with, and she'd pay nannies to raise our fantastic children.

Once they had left the nest, we'd both be back out on the world stage having adventures until our bodies told us to take it easy. Then we'd retire, spoil our grandkids rotten, and eventually die peacefully and pain-free surrounded by our super-successful, handsome family. Donna was very particular about the details and seemed very focused on her life goals.

How we were going to afford all this on my meager fifteen dollars an hour was beyond me. It definitely felt like we were on the clock. She'd always ask about my work and the prospects for advancement, and aggressively encourage me to do something, anything, with my script writing.

My page was mostly blank, and only had designs on staying at the call center. Climbing up the corporate ladder didn't interest me, and traveling the world? Shit, that would mean getting on a plane. Fuck. That.

The script writing was just a hobby, a silly pipe dream. A little creative outlet and never destined to be a career. If anyone wanted to pay me for one of my stories, I'd likely think they were joking or mad, and then have a panic attack.

We had discussed all this before marriage, and I guess I had halfheartedly agreed to all her demands, but why wouldn't I? She was attractive, and more critically, somehow interested in me. She said I "had a spark," whatever that meant. A hidden talent? A superpower? I was just glad she thought I had something worth exploring because entering my forties still unmarried was starting to depress me.

After our short honeymoon, the reality of everything I had signed up for hit me like an ACME anvil, and I found it hard to move onward and upward. The call center was my safe-space, and I found it easy to put all that Donna-life stuff on hold. It wasn't like I didn't like the idea of making more money and moving into a bigger place, I just couldn't make myself care about it. A horrible nervous energy would run through my body when I contemplated a change in career. And this would be followed by the feeling that if I did stick my neck out, everyone would find out I was an idiot. At the call center, I knew what was expected of me, and I was reliable and good with our customers.

Donna was big on going to the gym, something I was always impressed by and eternally grateful for. She'd come back to the apartment after a workout, rocking her leggings and tank top, with her long black hair tied back into a ponytail. She always looked fantastic after a workout. The woman glistened.

During the first few months of our marriage, she'd get back and I'd be greeted with a beautiful smile and a sweet sweaty kiss. As our marriage wore on—especially if she found me with a twenty-five-ounce Bud Light can in my hand—her welcome would be more formal and eventually, she wouldn't say anything.

In an attempt to prove I wasn't a complete lost cause, I loudly announced I would sign up for a class at the local gym. I picked a yoga class. I mean really, why not, right?

Lots of pose-striking and relaxing and stuff, it almost sounded bearable, and it seemed to impress Donna, a little. If "It's a start" was anything to feel good about.

For the first couple of weeks, everything went well. I'd spend an hour posing and relaxing and then go home and talk about it with Donna. I wouldn't say perfect marital bliss was restored, but I think she was happy that I seemed to be enjoying myself and was doing something outside of my comfort zone. I wasn't happy about it, but that wasn't the point. I was trying to take the easiest path away from appearing like a complete disappointment as a husband. My plan seemed to be working. Until week three.

Yoga was a breeze. With only an hour to work with, my class would strike a few simple poses, and then we'd spend the last twenty minutes relaxing. We'd be cats, cows, dogs, chairs, cobras, and even corpses. I mean seriously, I went to the gym and pretended to be a corpse. How perfect was this plan?

The one position I enjoyed the most was the legs-up-the-wall pose, which was exactly as named. Lay down, legs straight up, and hold for a few minutes. After that, we'd cross our legs and let the blood and muscles become properly reacquainted again. It felt fantastic!

If only all our positions were that invigorating.

Most of them made me feel stupid. Downward dog, cow, and cat should have been called, "Hey, look at my ass," "Do you see my ass?" and "That's no space station, that's an ASS!" It was also hard not to stare, or avoid, some of the specimens on display in the room, never mind stress about what my gelatinous rear end looked like to the unlucky asshole behind me.

Things came to a head when a new pose, "Say hello to my big ass," was introduced to the class. We were told to lay on our backs, and place our hands on the floor by our sides. Then, in one swift move, we would lift our legs and torso so that the tips of our toes were touching the floor behind our heads. Miss Bendy Instructor demonstrated, and of course, she made it look easy.

After watching the demonstration, I was suddenly very cognizant of the beef and bean burrito I ate before class, and the growing pressure looking to be relieved. I knew the whole point of this yoga class was to stretch and relax our muscles, but I had given strict instructions to certain areas of my body to do no such thing. They were to remain clenched, at all times, no matter what.

I couldn't get into the position, and typically, I was the only one in class with this problem. While everyone else lifted and set, my legs would lift and then fall to the floor. I tried kicking my legs, but it looked like I was riding an invisible upside-down bike. I tucked my legs against my belly and then tried to flick my feet backward, hoping the momentum would carry me over. It didn't work, and as I flailed about, I got more frustrated, and as I got more frustrated, I got embarrassed. I could feel my face getting redder, and I could hear other people in the room laughing at me. Fucking yoga elites.

My torso was the problem. It was too long. Girls in high school would frequently say, "He looks weird. The top half of his body is too long," and Miss Bendy confirmed this as I rolled around trying to get into "Say hello to my big ass": "You have a long torso. This position will be difficult."

Really? No shit!

I hated my body, from its beer-fueled belly to its skinny arms and legs. I was weirdly kind of thin and kind of fat at the same time. Thank goodness for that "spark," right?

I formulated a new plan to get into, "Say hello to my big ass." I leaned forward and then quickly rolled my whole body backward. As my back hit the floor, I threw my legs toward my head, and it worked. The momentum in my legs dragged my torso into the air, and my feet touched the floor above my head. There was only one problem. I had forgotten all about my clenching responsibilities.

It was the strangest fart I had ever done. The gas didn't just leak out in a steady stream, creating an embarrassing sound and smell. It just left. All of it, in one loud, massive bang. The force of it actually hurt my sphincter muscle. It was so surprising I suddenly sounded like a member of the English gentry and shouted, "Excuse me!" Then I lost my balance and crashed to the floor in a heap of methane scented failure.

Everyone in the class freaking lost it. Bodies collapsed all over the gym as everyone laughed. Tears streamed down faces, fingers pointed in my direction, and reenactments were performed. Even Miss Bendy had lost her composure.

I rapidly looked at each person in turn, willing them to stop. The sound of their laughter seemed to echo off the walls and double up in my ears. They kept laughing. Pointing.

I got to my feet and ran to the exit and, of course, pulled on the door that wanted to be pushed. I panicked and couldn't figure out what to do. "Push." Push what? Damn it! As I pulled harder, the little voice inside my head started to pick on me. *You fucked up again.* I know. *You should have never taken that stupid class.* I know. *Time for a beer.* I know.

VII.

Sherryl delivers my chicken-fried steak, and my new body lets out a little fart in anticipation of the carbs and fat I'm about to devour. At least my intestinal track is still working in a familiar way. Maybe this isn't a dream after all, and I am, in fact, dead. If I'm honest, it's not like any dream I've had before.

My dreams are usually a mishmash of desires and worries, a collage of things that need to be understood and compartmentalized. They didn't stay in one location for long—certainly not as long as I've been in this Denny's restaurant—and they never felt as real as this Denny's does right now.

The worst dreams, okay, nightmares, were always one of two overwhelming experiences. I was either stuck at work in an uncontrollable call center or playing tennis with a pear-shaped alien. I'm not sure where my brain got the idea of a pear-shaped alien—it didn't resemble anything I'd ever read about or watched on television—but it would calmly fire tennis balls from his pear-shaped arms at me faster than I could hit back. I would wake up after a tennis ball smashed into my face.

The call center nightmares came later in life after I started working there. These were much more straightforward and resembled a horrible day at work. I would be overwhelmed with calls, and my phone would be huge and cover the entire width of my desk, with all fifty lines demanding my attention. I would wake up from these dreams after a customer forced his or her way into the call center and punched me in the face.

"Why are you lying to yourself about the yoga class?" Taylor asks. "No one laughed."

"Yes, they did."

"No, they didn't. The other people in the classroom heard you pass wind, but no one made fun of you."

"They did. I distinctly remember my class laughing at me."

"Mr. Pringate. I'm not going to debate the point because I know I'm right. That event in your life is recorded, and it didn't play out the way you remember it. I shouldn't be surprised that you don't recall it correctly. The way humans recall memories is unreliable and often rewritten to suit an individual's internal narrative. But for argument's sake, I'll play along with your little fantasy. Why then couldn't you see the humor in that event?"

Disregarding all that other crap—I know what I know— I did eventually look back on that night and laugh about it. Everything gets clearer in hindsight, once you have time to analyze the event. As I often did in painstaking detail along with all the other moments in my life where I'd fallen on my ass or said the wrong thing. It was like having a Rolodex organizing my fuckups from A to Z, always ready to be revisited with no resolution possible.

"Yeah, well, I panicked," I say.

I grab the napkin wrapped around my knife and fork and unravel. My food smells excellent—a massive slab of beef covered in batter, fried to perfection, and smothered with gravy, served with potatoes and toast. Sherryl is correct; this is my favorite.

"Okay, so if this isn't a dream, then what is that circle above the diagram?" I ask.

"That is where we are right now," she says.

"That's not very helpful." I slice a big chunk of fat-covered meat and shoehorn it into my mouth.

Taylor looks a little horrified as I chew my food and breathe heavily through my nose.

"What I mean to say is, this isn't Earth, and it isn't the good or bad place. This," she uses both hands to point all around us, "is a kind of holding area. In terms that might make more sense to you, this is like a Holodeck."

"From Star Trek?"

"Pretty much, only this one is much bigger and way more sophisticated," she says.

I push some of the gravy off my steak onto the potatoes and then scoop the gooey mixture up and into my mouth with my fork. Taylor again looks a little horrified. I'm enjoying her reactions, so I consider chewing with my mouth open. I point at the window and the white fog with my knife. "Doesn't seem that big."

"It'll get bigger."

I can't help myself; I start to chew with my mouth open. I'm such a child.

Taylor looks down at her notes and continues, "Right now your evaluation area is being built from your memories, such as they are, and from the information we have on the area and the people that live here. When it's complete, and we're ready to begin, everything you see beyond this restaurant will look, feel, and smell like the Anaheim, California, you grew up in."

"Okay, and then what?" I ask.

Taylor looks up and smiles. "Then the hunt begins."

For a moment I choke on my food, but manage to swallow and wash everything down with some coffee. "The what?"

"Yes, Mr. Pringate. The hunt. We're going to hunt you down. Well, a representative from the shitty place is anyway. He's on his way to kill you, so we can't dawdle."

I suddenly lose my appetite, and I put my cutlery down on the table. "Kill me? But I thought you said I was already dead."

"You are, but this is all part of the game. This is your last chance to make something of yourself. To prove there's more to you than the twenty-four/seven sameness. To show you can live and appreciate life."

Just as I thought I was starting to get a handle on this stupid situation, she starts confusing me again. Live life after death? Could I die twice?

"You have to admit everything you just said sounded crazy, right?"

Taylor leans forward and folds her arms. "I realize this is a lot to take in, but trust me, you don't want to get killed here."

"Why? I am already dead. I mean, what is this Hell like anyway?"

"Hell and Heaven actually both look a lot like Earth, just with a few specific differences."

I grab my knife and fork again and angrily attack my food. Now I'm stress eating. "Okay, explain."

"Remember the Venn diagram. Earth sits in the middle where both good and bad exist. You must have had a bad day or two, and maybe the occasional day that didn't suck. Well, try to remember everything that happened to you on a bad day. Maybe you stubbed your toe, burnt your toast, hit every red light on the way to work, arrived late for a meeting, and in your case specifically, maybe all your calls at work were from angry customers. That's Hell on Earth. That's what's waiting for you if you screw this up."

Okay, that did sound pretty bad, and not the biblical torture we, as Christians, had been promised. I'd had days like that, and as much as I liked the call center, there were times when some stupid thing had gone wrong with shipping on our company website, and I had to listen to the complaints. "That doesn't sound completely awful."

"It gets worse. It's not just the occasional day that happens; it's every day. Every single day, events will conspire to put you in a bad mood. Just when you think you've had a bit of luck, it'll be snatched away and replaced with something truly shitty. You'll get angry, every day, and eventually, you'll get so miserable you'll try to kill yourself, only to find you can't. You'll wake up in your bed as if nothing had happened, and the whole process will start again. Basically, all the most depressing parts of the movie *Groundhog Day*. You'll also look and feel terrible, all the time. The injuries suffered in life will revisit you from time to time. Old wounds will occasionally open up and bleed, then get infected, then heal. Again, and again. That place is tears, pain, and depression, baked into a cake made of misery and despair."

I stop eating again. "And the good place?"

"Exactly the opposite. The good place isn't winning the lottery and being filthy rich, or anything stupid like that. It's finding the last Snickers bar in the vending machine. It's green lights all the way to work, and a job you love. It's friends in the office remembering your birthday with a surprise cake. If you pull this off Mr. Pringate, you'll help a friend decorate their house and feel appreciated, right before having the best night's sleep of your life. You'll happily pull over to help someone stranded at the side of the road. This version of what you'd call Heaven will be meet-cutes, beautiful sunsets, and playing with puppies. Each day is like the last act of an outstanding romantic comedy, a little bit of drama, followed by a glorious life-affirming moment. It's always fresh, always shiny and new."

The old saying about when something "sounds like it's too good to be true" plays in my head, and then I remember something Taylor said. "Hold on; you said someone could be stranded at the side of the road. If they're in Heaven with me, why would they break down?"

"Good question. I'm glad you're paying attention. Go back to the Venn diagram. The two places overlap. Not everything is hellish in Hell, and it's not all cute kittens in Heaven. The difference is, that person who broke down in Heaven will meet you, and you'll likely become great friends or even lovers. In Hell, if someone pulls over to help you with a flat tire, they'll fix it, and then walk off with your tools after kicking you in the balls."

I arrange my knife and fork on the plate to indicate I'm done eating and push it to the center of the table. I think Taylor understands I need a moment and she looks over the notes in her binder again.

There's still nothing beyond the white fog outside. I imagine the fog will eventually clear and reveal the street. It'll look normal, and I wonder what would happen if I just get up and leave the restaurant. It would be nice to forget that I'm dead. It would be nice to go home, crack open a beer, and watch cartoons. Let the crisp golden liquid smooth away my anxieties and turn off the world, if only for a moment.

"How did I die?" I ask.

"I can't tell you."

"Why not?"

"It's something we like to leave to the deceased to find out. You can play detective if you like. This space is like a sandbox for you to play in and look back on your life. This little mystery can be your project while we conduct your evaluation."

"How did you end up here?"

"I, unlike everyone else you'll meet, didn't end up here. I was never on Earth. Think of me as a manifestation of the universal energy. Not really the right hand, but more like a picky finger on the right hand. Any ideas as to how you might have died?"

I say the first thing that enters my head.

"I bet it was Donna."

VIII.

My marriage didn't end quietly.

I could tell Donna was getting more and more irritated with my lack of ambition. We had moved past extended periods of silent disapproval and downgraded to barely audible mumblings of dissatisfaction. After the yoga debacle, I vowed to never sign up for another gym class ever again. I took my epic failure as a sign that I shouldn't have ventured outside my comfort zone.

At this point in our marriage, barely two years in, sex didn't happen, and we'd stopped going out. I found myself equally scared of addressing the issues we had and the consequences of doing nothing. On days when things were relatively cordial, I would consider sitting her down to talk about our relationship, but I would always chicken out. What would be the point anyway? I knew what the problem was; it was me. Why screw up a perfectly good day to explore that?

On bad days, I'd keep my distance—which was hard to do in a one-bedroom apartment—so as not to aggravate the situation and make matters worse. It was a cowardly strategy, I knew it, but at the same time, I was able to rationalize it into a positive. No drama equaled staying together. A few beers would always smooth away the edges either way. At the end of another successful week of avoiding the issue I would say to myself, "Well, I'm still married," right before cracking open another brew to celebrate.

When Donna was unhappy about something, she wouldn't talk about it right away. She'd let her feelings fester and build like magma in a volcano, and there'd be little warning of the explosion to come. When the pressure exceeded her ability to hold it all in, she let me know in no uncertain terms. "You're a soulless, boring, lazy sonofabitch!"

Donna slapped the cold twenty-five ounce can of Bud Light out of my hand. The nearly full container smacked against the fence bordering our patio and sprayed beer everywhere.

She continued her attack. Each word punctuated with a fist as she continued. "I can't believe I wasted two years on you. Why do I always pick the losers? I'm such an idiot!"

I raised my arms to protect myself. Donna's time at the gym was then something I despised as she repeatedly tried to punch through my arms to get to my head. Damn, she was strong. I fell off my chair, and she started to kick me. She wasn't fussy about where—my back, ass, and legs were all equal-opportunity targets.

"Mark my words, you worthless piece of shit. You're gonna pay for this. I'm going to make sure this breakup hurts!"

Donna marched back into the apartment, and I could hear things being thrown around. The smashing glass was probably my collection of pint glasses. The sound of snapping plastic was likely my old collection of vinyl records. I slowly climbed back onto my chair as hurricane

Donna exited my life. Several areas of my body were reporting injuries.

She reappeared at the door to the apartment, holding another of my big beers and her packed suitcase. I ducked and covered under the patio table.

"You are so pathetic." She opened the can of beer and emptied it over the table. The foamy liquid poured through the gaps in the table top and then down all over me. "You'll be hearing from me, asshole."

She leaned over and threw the empty can at me. It somehow broke through my defenses and hit my forehead. A vicious "full-stop" to end this chapter of my life.

Once she had gone, I rolled over onto my back and placed my hands on my belly. I looked up at the night sky through the gaps in the table. The last morsels of beer dripped down, and I caught a few in my mouth.

I could hear muffled conversations on nearby patios. Our tightly packed community of strangers was likely intrigued by the ruckus and was now passing judgment on my beer-soaked, beaten body lying under a table.

What struck me the most was how relieved I was. This was at least an end to the daily analysis, and the "should I?", "shouldn't I?" say something. Everything seemed settled, for the moment, and my options going forward were now simpler. All that stuff about the only woman I've ever loved walking out the door could wait. I knew what I had to do.

I got up and walked into my apartment. I wasn't curious about the damage Donna had done. I could see pieces of my record collection on the floor, and I did keep an eye on where I was placing my feet to avoid any pieces of glass. I opened my fridge and was relieved to see the rest of my beer was still waiting for me. I grabbed one and went back outside.

The first gulp felt crisp against my throat, and by the third mouthful, I could feel the tension in my shoulders drop. I was aware I stank of beer, but I didn't care. I was happy to be embraced by my favorite thing, inside and out. All thoughts of a pending divorce and Donna's threats were pushed to the back in my mind, and I wondered if the remaining beers I had were going to be enough. If I quickly showered and changed, I could walk to one of my liquor stores and pick up a couple more cans. I had three stores within walking distance, and I'd rotate my visits so as not to seem too regular. Once back at my apartment, I'd watch one of my favorite movies as I drank myself into a coma.

My plan for the rest of my evening was set, and I was excited to get started. I would deal with the shitty reality of my life tomorrow.

IX.

"So, Donna is your number one suspect?" Taylor asks. "That seems reasonable considering how your relationship ended."

"She did have it in for me. She got even more pissed off when she went after half my shit and discovered half my shit was less than nothing. I guess I don't have to worry about the divorce now since I'm dead."

Sherryl visits our table again, refills my coffee cup, and takes away my plate.

"So, what happens now?"

"Well, I have to make some selections here, and then you're good to go."

"Selections?"

"Yes, you didn't think we'd send you out there alone, did you?"

"I'm not sure what I expected. I've never been dead before. Who are you selecting to help me? Do I get a vote? Schwarzenegger's Commando or Stallone's Rambo could be useful."

Taylor moves to another section of her binder.

"I'm not going to tell you. It'll be a surprise. Besides, I can only pick from the deceased. I'll make the selections; you need to think about your investigation and everything else we've talked about."

As I think about my failed marriage, and its impending end, I feel heavier, smaller. Self-deprecation was never a problem for me. Despite how I may have acted, I did love Donna, even if she didn't love me. If I had my spark, she was most certainly a Heaven-sent bolt of lightning in my life. I think about all the times I drank myself into a coma halfway through one of my favorite movies. I'd sometimes wake up as she—clearly disappointed—shut down the entertainment system and the living room lights. She'd order me to stay on the couch if I tried to stagger into the bedroom. That was most of the time. Sometimes I'd just quietly drink, space out, and then pass out. Occasionally I'd put on my headphones and cry as I sang along to my favorite songs. Every once in a while, the booze would unlock the darkness and Donna would be burdened with my ugliest fears and plans. I wouldn't remember anything I said or did the next morning. Donna's mood the next day would give me a clue as to how far I went.

After we separated, I heard she had found herself an apartment nearby and was likely looking for another Mr. Right again. I wonder how she killed me? I don't think she owned a gun or even knew how to use one. I guess she could have simply beat me to death with a baseball bat or something, but I suspect Donna would do something a little smarter than that. She'd probably arrange a horrible accident for me, or try to poison me somehow. This train of thought inspires another question for Taylor.

"When you die, are there any marks left on your afterlife body?"

I unbutton my shirt so that I can get a better look at the new me. Maybe there is a scar from a bullet wound or where Donna stabbed me.

"No, well, not immediately anyway," says Taylor. "As I said before, if you don't make it through this, you'll take any injuries you picked up with you, and look as you did on Earth. Put your shirt back on. This version of you right now is the mental projection of the ideal you."

"Huh? I've never looked like this."

Taylor picks up the chrome napkin holder on the table and hands it to me with the flat, shiny back pointed at my face. I have to admit, I do see something of myself in the person reflected.

She continues, "This face, that body, is what you could have looked like if you had just made a few different life choices. It's the best version of you. Being that you're about to be hunted, we use the you that'll best serve you as we process your evaluation. The actual you wouldn't last five minutes."

"Really?" I ask.

"Seriously. The guy from Hell is no joke."

"And I'm just supposed to shoot this guy or something?"

"Well, you could. But this isn't going to be that easy. Shooting someone you know is already dead hardly proves anything. We're not that easily fooled. We'll be looking deeper than that. For a real change in your thinking."

Taylor finds what she was looking for in her binder. She pulls out a sheet of paper from its sleeve; it looks like some kind of form. She checks three boxes and signs an area at the bottom of the page.

She holds up the paper, and it disappears in a flash and pop of blue electrical light.

"Right, Mr. Pringate. Excited?"

"Not really. More scared than anything else."

"Well, that's not a surprise. If you were, we'd probably wouldn't need to do all this."

Taylor looks out the window by our booth. I follow her gaze and notice the white fog is changing. It's taking on flashes of color; blues and reds mix in with the white. The intensity of the light gets stronger as its source gets closer to the restaurant. The frequency of the flashing lights seems familiar.

At first, there's no sound from outside; then, as the entire restaurant becomes completely surrounded by the blue and red flashing lights, I hear a screech of tires and the unmistakable blast of police sirens.

"What's going on?" I ask. I shuffle out of the booth.

"You're being taken into custody," says Taylor.

"Arrested? What for?"

"Nothing. But we need to get you out of here."

Several armed police officers storm into the restaurant as the fog outside clears. Denny's is surrounded by police cars. As the fog moves further away, I see the street, and a few people gather to get a better look at the drama unfolding inside the restaurant.

"Down on the ground, now!" one officer yells at me. He's joined by the rest of his team, very much wanting me to find the floor. I drop like a sack of potatoes.

"Hands on your head."

I comply again and throw in a "Yes, sir. No problem, sir." for good measure.

The officer who yelled at me first holsters his gun. He walks over to me and places a knee on my back. He then forces my hands behind my back, and I hear what must be handcuffs click into place around my wrists. They feel tight against my skin.

"Good luck, Mr. Pringate," says Taylor.

I start to panic. "Look, I don't want to do this. I lived an okay life, right? I wasn't that bad; I didn't steal. It's not like I ever killed anyone!"

I'm lifted off the ground by my very strong arresting officer. Taylor walks over and stands in front of us.

"That's not the point, Mr. Pringate. Earth is a rare gem in the universe. A planet capable of supporting life. A human life is even rarer, a sentient lifeform capable of dazzling dreams and invention. Your time on Earth was an incredibly precious thing, Mr. Pringate, and you wasted it. Use this experience to look back at your life, see where you could have embraced adventure. Try to change and take some risks, and most importantly, be honest with yourself. Or else face the consequences."

Taylor steps closer to me and pokes me in the chest with her finger. "This is your last chance, Pringate. This is the beginning of your afterlife, flashing before our eyes. We'll be watching you." She points at the ceiling. I glance up and only see a ceiling fan, then assume she means the entire universe. No pressure then.

"Don't fuck it up." Taylor steps aside and the officer, holding my collar and bound wrists, marches me outside. I complain some more, but no one is listening to me. It seems I'm in this game whether I want to be or not. The idea that I'm going to be hunted scares the shit out of me. The thought of spending eternity on a crappy version of Earth scares the shit out of me.

I want to go home.

Chapter 2: One Step

I.

I'm led away from Denny's to a waiting police car. I'm surprised and a little excited to see that it's an old Dodge Monaco sedan, the freaking Bluesmobile! The back passenger's side door is opened, and my arresting officer forces me to take a seat while also encouraging me not to bang my head on the door frame. He walks around to the other side of the car and joins me. Two more officers jump into the front.

The car, unsurprisingly, smells old, like a newspaper at the bottom of a negligent owner's birdcage. An air freshener, shaped like a Christmas tree, hanging from the rearview mirror is only making things worse. The car smells like pine-scented bird poop, like someone took a dump on Christmas.

The car's seats have seen plenty of action too. They are covered in a horrible, shiny black vinyl, which is pitted and cracked. As I awkwardly try to get comfortable with my hands still cuffed, I see some of the seams have given up, and stained orange foam is beginning to escape.

"We'll keep you restrained until we reach the station," says my arresting officer. "We never know if you Fresh Deaths are going to make a run for it or not. I'm Officer Jones, up front driving is Officer Cartwright. The ugly bastard next to him is Officer Smith." The two men nonchalantly wave without turning around. They scan the surrounding area, and Officer Jones turns in his seat to keep an eye on the road behind us.

Officer Cartwright puts the car into drive, and we take off down Tustin Street.

"Am I under arrest or not?" I ask.

"Not really. But we are going to put you in a holding cell until your first counselor arrives," says Jones.

"Counselor? Oh, that's right. The people sent to help me. Do you know who they're sending?"

"No clue."

Officer Smith jumps into the conversation. "How many boxes did your Transition Consultant check?"

I think back to the piece of paper that Taylor held up before it got zapped into non-existence. "Three, I think."

"Wow, that's unusual. You're going to get up to three counselors, depending on how you do," says Smith. "Your Transition Consultant is in control of everything here. He or she—"

Jones interrupts, "It's Taylor."

The three officers momentarily go quiet and exchange a glance. Something about Taylor clearly disturbs them.

I have to ask, "What? What's wrong with Taylor?"

Smith shrugs. "Nothing."

I can tell he's holding something back.

Jones continues, "Don't worry about it, she's great. You're in good hands. She arranged this police escort, which means she's taking your case very seriously. Not everyone gets an entire police department's protection."

Jones takes a quick left onto Lincoln Avenue. The officers continue to keep an eye out on the road up front and behind, as though they're expecting trouble at any second. The street looks normal enough. A regular sunny day in California. A collage of beige walls, the gleam off store windows, big colorful logos, sprinklers desperately trying to keep grass green in a desert, and the occasional palm tree. Perfectly familiar, except there are no other cars on the road, and no one walking about.

I wonder if there's a politically correct way to approach the subject of death. I imagine it's a touchy subject here in the afterlife, so I have to be careful. "So . . . are you guys dead?" *That didn't sound good at all.*

The three officers exchange another glance before Jones answers. "Yes."

The next question is obvious, but I'm not feeling brave enough to ask. Officer Smith, thankfully, makes things easy for me.

"I was killed in the line of duty. Officer Cartwright here made it to retirement and died of natural causes, and Jones—"

"—Jones is none of your business—"

"—A bungee jumping accident." Smith laughs. "Perfectly good bridge, didn't check his equipment, jumps off, splat."

Jones shakes his head, and Cartwright chuckles.

I look again at the three men. They all seem to be in their late thirties to me, like every supporting actor I've ever seen on *T. J. Hooker.*

"But you all made it to Heaven, right?" I ask.

Jones answers. "Of course. All cops do. Well, most of us. Let me put it this way; you have to really fuck up as a cop not to end up on the right side of the universe. Same goes for firefighters, nurses, soldiers. If you put yourself out there and try to do some good in the world, you're pretty much set."

"Who doesn't make it, generally?" I ask.

Cartwright spoke first. "The usual suspects. Lawyers, Wall Street types."

"Politicians, especially the ones that have been in office for more than one term," Jones adds.

"CEOs, most of the big stars in Hollywood," Smith says.

"And maybe, you, if you don't take advantage of this opportunity." Jones gives me a serious look.

"Yeah, maybe," I say.

We take a left onto South Harbor Boulevard and just past the public library I see the Anaheim Police Department. The massive red brick building sits amongst tall palm trees and beautifully manicured lawns. I see a "Go Ducks!" sign hanging from the roof.

"Okay, get ready, Pringate. When I tell you to move, move. Run straight for the lobby and keep your head down," says Jones.

We pull into the visitors parking lot and skid to a halt outside the building's main entrance. Jones jumps out of the car and runs around to my side. My door is opened, and I'm pulled out by my collar. Cartwright and Smith step outside the vehicle, their guns drawn, and they begin scanning the area.

As best I can with my hands behind my back, I run toward the main entrance. I can feel Jones' hand push against my back, which isn't helping me keep my balance. Once inside, Jones closes and locks the doors. I turn around and see that Cartwright and Smith haven't moved.

I'm pushed past the visitor waiting room. It's empty, save for a corkboard loaded with helpful public notices. Jones herds me toward the front desk. The officer behind the counter seems clued in on the situation and lets us through a security door to our left. Jones is careful to make sure the door closes and locks behind us.

We march down a corridor through the main office. Through the windows, I can see police and what looks like regular office staff getting ready for a war. Each is loading and checking their weapons. A young woman hands out body armor from a cart.

"What's going on?" I ask.

"The rep from Hell is on his way for you. If he gets here before your first counselor, we'll try to hold him off for as long as we can," says Jones.

I'm led through another security door and down to the holding cells. I can feel my heart racing. This situation is starting to feel real, and I hate that all this drama is because of me. I hate being the center of attention.

We reach the holding cells. Officer Jones opens the thick metal door of the last cell at the end of the corridor and pushes me inside. He takes out his keys and unlocks my cuffs. I rub my wrists where the cold metal has pinched my skin and left a mark.

"Stay here and don't move," says Jones. "The only way out is the way we came in. Hopefully your counselor will get here first, but if not, take this."

Jones holds out a small gun. I don't know what type it is. I don't take it.

"This is a Glock 17. I'm chambering a round." He pulls back on the gun and I hear a double click, just like in the movies, and then he places it on the cot inside my cell. "If you want to get involved, just pick it up and come join us. It's easy, just point and pull the trigger."

I look at the gun for a second and then at Jones. *He's got to be kidding, right?* He winks at me. *What's that all about?*

"Can you tell me who my counselor is?" I ask.

Jones stands in the doorway to my cell, at first holding out his hand to me like he's commanding a dog not to follow him, but then he shrugs like he's changed his mind. "Just stay in that cell if you want, or not, okay?" Jones runs down the hall and out of sight. I hear a heavy door slam shut.

For several minutes I'm left alone with my thoughts. I stand across the room from my cot and the Glock pistol. I've never owned a gun before, never wanted to. For a brief moment I wonder how heavy it feels, then I stop caring as other concerns push to the front of my mind. I'm a dead man, and now prey, being punished for what? Being boring? Drinking too much? Wasn't it my life to live how I liked? I wasn't a bad person. Until this ride in the infamous Bluesmobile, I'd never seen the inside of a police car. I hadn't broken any laws. If I knew there was some damn sentient space energy keeping score, I might have made more of an effort.

Now I have to figure out how to do, what exactly? Zig instead of zag? Do the opposite of me? Be a better person? I didn't think the man upstairs, or whatever it is, was this nuanced with his punishments. From what I remember of the Bible, he was strictly a thumbs up or thumbs down kind of omnipotent being; there was no afterlife sandbox for people to figure things out and get in touch with their feelings.

Thoughts of escape fill my mind. I think about all those remote places I looked at on the computer over the years and what it must be like to live there. The roads less traveled, or a point on the freeway where you can stop and feel like the only person on the planet.

I often lose myself in daydreams and fantasize about living in a house, miles away from people. Somewhere I could feel safe and watch the seasons slowly come and go from my wrap around porch. A place where I wouldn't have to concern myself with other people's judgments or watch people I love become old and die. It would be nice to have that barrier against the world and choose when and where and how I connect with it.

My stupor is interrupted by the sound of what could only be gunfire in the police station. I hear muffled pops and bangs first, then some rapid fire from further away in the building—two sides of a violent argument. As each side shouts, I notice the pops and bangs take longer to respond, and there are less of them. The conversation becomes one-sided as the louder, faster weapon silences more voices. I hear furniture crash and glass break. It sounds like the Pops and Bangs are losing.

I think I'm on team Pops and Bangs. *Fuck!*

I look at the Glock again, but I can't bring myself to pick it up. I try to ignore the sounds of the gunfight getting closer to my cell. My hands start to shake. I fold my arms and wedge my hands under my armpits to keep them still.

There's one final drumroll of gunfire, and then every-thing gets real quiet.

I step out into the corridor. I still don't hear anything. Wondering if I can leave, I make my way toward the exit. It feels like several minutes have gone by, but it may have only been a few seconds. The only thing marking the passage of time is the sound of blood pumping in my ears. Each pulse is a new second, and each deep breath marks a new minute.

The door is hidden around a corner, so I carefully take a look to see what's what—so far so good. The security door is shut. I crouch down and sneak up to the window to get a better look at the corridor outside. Craning my head around the small window, I try to study as much of the space as possible.

On the floor, I can see spent bullet casings, and the punctured walls tell the story of an epic battle. The air is still misty with smoke, but I don't see any bodies or blood anywhere.

Keeping an eye on the corridor I reach down and try the door handle, but I freeze when a new face meets mine on the other side of the glass. The pulsing in my ear stops, or at least I don't notice it anymore. I hold my breath.

His piercing black eyes are fixed on me. His slim face is the color and texture of cigarette ash. He smiles and reveals receding gums with long yellow teeth that are a turd brown color near the roots. The black hair on his head is a patchwork of wispy growths and bald spots, a sorry collection of tiny combovers glued to his scalp with grease. Blood trickles down the sides of his face from open wounds in his temples. He speaks. His voice somehow reaches through the door and bypasses my ears to form the words inside my mind.

"This is so disappointing, Mr. Pringate. This little game over so soon."

I remember to breathe again and gasp for air.

"Taylor is going to be so disappointed with you."

The mention of Taylor's name helps ground me a little. "Taylor?"

"Yes, she's not had a good run lately. Her last client ended up in Hell. You can call me Eugene, by the way."

~~The Devil's~~ Eugene's words sound muffled through the door and no longer boom inside my head. His demeanor has also changed—less demon from the beyond and more, Mr. Greed-Is-Good-Gordon-Gekko from the movie *Wall Street*. He still looks like a meth addict that had fallen asleep in an ashtray, though. "You know, I think you'll like it."

"Like what?"

"The Hell that awaits you."

"It didn't sound so good when Taylor talked about it. Have you seen yourself?"

Eugene smiles and shows me his pearly-yellows again. "I know I'm pretty. But look at it this way—everyone bleeds in Hell, and no one cares. Everyone's scars are out there for everyone to see. We're all just one big, carefree, happy family."

Eugene presses his forehead against the glass. "It's all freedom, you know? And no responsibility. You get to steal your cake and eat it. You can drink all day, every day, if you want to. You'd like that, wouldn't you, Pringate? Wouldn't you like the argument to end?"

I knew precisely what Eugene was talking about. The pressure that built and built, the debate that got louder and louder in my mind the more days I resisted a visit to one of my liquor stores. If I'd managed to go a full week without a beer, I'd most certainly cave on Friday after work. Just to make the headaches go away. Over the years I thought I had gotten it under control, and I tried to time my falls. I made sure I had nothing to do and nowhere to be after I woke up with a hangover. I'd sleep in and then start my day with an energy drink, followed by coffee before making myself a bacon sandwich. It was my bullshit ritual that I had convinced myself was the cure for the common hangover. Every week I did this. My little routine. I patted myself on the back for finding an equilibrium between the daily pressure, and the few hours I got to tune the world out.

"So, are you going to come quietly? Or do I have to shoot you through the door?"

I don't get to decide.

A massive explosion erupts from my old cell at the end of the corridor. The blast shakes the building and knocks me off my feet. I cough as dust and debris cover me. From the darkness comes a new voice, a loud, booming, weirdly melodic voice.

"Holy shit! Corporal Green is making the jailhouse rock. Oh-huh! Thank you. Thank you very much." *Is that an Elvis impression?*

Boots stomp over broken concrete. Then a huge hand grabs me by my shirt and lifts me off the ground—Corporal Green speaks to Eugene.

"Sorry I'm late. The freeways in this theater are a logistical nightmare. Your doing?"

"Nope. Humans did that to themselves."

"Figures. Well, fuck off, Eugene, this kid ain't yours yet."

Corporal Green pushes me down the corridor toward my old cell. Then I hear a massive blast from a shotgun. I manage to restore sight in one eye before I'm pushed back into what's left of my cell. It's a lot brighter than before on account of the large hole in the back wall letting in the sunlight.

Beyond the cell, in the parking lot, stands a pristine 1977 Pontiac Firebird Trans Am. It's black. It has a fiery golden bird painted on the hood. It's the Bandit's car!

"Pick a seat, Pringate," offers Corporal Green.

I stagger over to the passenger's side and jump in, then wipe the dust out of my other eye to get a better look at my—what I assume is my—first counselor.

From the vantage point I have inside the car, all I can see are his camo-pants. Once he plops himself into the driver's seat, I get a better look at him.

"You didn't want to drive?" Corporal Green asks.

II.

It was the best, and yet, worst, test drive of my life.

I arrived at the Ford dealership looking to buy a car. I wasn't hopeful about which one because I knew I couldn't afford much. That put me firmly in the tiny car part of the dealership parking lot.

After a few probing questions from the over-the-top friendly car salesman—I was an easy mark since I didn't do any research or question anything—he selected a white Ford Focus with gray cloth seats, a compact disc player, and an automatic transmission. Apparently, this was in my price range, so I immediately gave up on any fancy notions of powered leather seats and satellite navigation.

We spent less than a minute going over the details of the car, which I figured was due to there being very few details to talk about. I was the proverbial lamb being calmly led to the slaughter, but now, somehow, I wanted this basic, no-fuss little car. That was my trunk I just inspected. Those were my tires I just kicked.

I got into the car, and the salesman took the passenger seat. We started *him* up (all my cars are a he and called R2, of R2D2 fame) and headed out into the street.

With each passing second, I liked the car more and more. I sat a little taller in my seat and breathed in the new-car smell. I may have been driving a piece of shit for all I knew, but I started to forgive its limitations as we drove on. There was no light next to the mirror glued to the sun visor. *Never mind, I didn't need that anyway.* The engine sounded a bit buzzy to me. *That's probably because it's fuel efficient.* It didn't have Bluetooth. *But it had an AUX port, so that's okay.* I loved this car, and I started to figure out how much extra a month I could afford to pay to make sure it was mine. No way was I letting this baby get away from me.

We were driving down North Tustin Street, and the salesman instructed me to take a right on East Heim Avenue. At the end of Heim I was told to make a right onto North Canal Street. I figured we'd find and make another right onto Lincoln Avenue and head back to Tustin Street. I was correct.

As we approached Tustin Street again, I was already in the right lane ready to head back to the dealership. I waited for an opening and took the turn, right into the passenger's side door of an old green Honda Civic. It must have shot through the red light on the other side of the road. I didn't see it coming.

The Civic's momentum coupled with the nudge from my car caused it to skid to a halt about twenty feet away. The salesman and I just sat there in shock. The Civic didn't move either. It was like the real world got kicked into the future and we all needed to catch up. When normal time resumed, our little test drive quickly turned into a Rallycross tour!

"He's getting away," shouted my salesman. "Get after him."

At first, in the panic, I didn't know what he meant. *Get him. Get who?* Then it clicked.

"Chase him?" We just assumed it was a guy. "No way."

The salesman unbuckled his seatbelt and then pressed the red button on mine.

"Then get out of the way. I want that asshole's plate number."

Why I didn't just leave the car and walk to the dealership I'll never figure out. Maybe I had bonded with the little compact car, and I wanted to see what it could do.

I climbed onto the back seat. Once there, I struggled with my new belt as the now injured, but brave Ford Focus lurched forward to pursue the cowardly Civic.

The chase was on. I managed to click my belt in place as the salesman simultaneously followed the Civic onto the 55 freeway, and dialed 911 on his flip phone. I could see the Civic weave in and out of traffic on the entry ramp, but it was no match for my new Focus. The salesman clearly understood how to unlock my car's impressive potential and easily kept up with our hit-and-run driver. My car's engine, however, was now making a loud rattling noise.

Out on the freeway, traffic was thankfully light.

"Hello, 911?" said my salesman. Wasn't it weird that people confirm that number? It was only three digits and very hard to fuck up. "Good. I'd like to report a hit and run."

Since the Civic had reached the freeway first, it had put a little distance between us. My car soon caught up.

The salesman continued. "I don't have time to give you my name and number. Let me give you the license plate first. Hold on."

The Civic headed toward the freeway exit at Katella Ave. The speedometer told me we were doing eighty-five miles an hour to keep up. The Civic driver headed down the ramp and even put on his blinkers to tell us he was planning to turn right onto the road. Both cars slowed down as the street approached.

At the last moment, the Civic lurched straight across the center of the street and jumped back onto the freeway. The salesman was able to do the same, narrowly avoiding another car. He slammed his foot on the accelerator and once again pulled the Civic back in. We were now in visual range of the license plate.

"Ready for the number?" said the salesman. "It's two, golf, alpha, tango, one, two, three."

I was impressed, and I wondered what my sales guy did before selling cars. Maybe he used to be a soldier or a cop? He certainly knew his way around that funky alphabet stuff. I keep meaning to learn it as it might come in handy at the call center.

He continued his conversation. "We're on the 55 heading south . . . Yes, we're following him . . . Oh, okay . . . Did you get the plate? Okay, we'll be back at the Ford dealership on Tustin Avenue."

The salesman stored his phone in one of my nicely sized cup holders and stopped pursuing the other car. We watched the green Civic continue down the freeway as we exited and headed back to the dealership.

"Well, that was fun," said the salesman.

Was it? I wondered if I could have made that drive. Probably not. There were several moments during the chase where I'm sure I would have crashed and killed us both. I probably did the right thing.

"So, how do you like the car?" he asked.

"It's great! I want it."

He laughed and nodded. "Don't worry; I have ten more just like this one back at the dealership."

For a moment, I was disappointed. I thought I would get this car. My car. The fantastic Civic hunter! But after giving it a bit of thought, I figured the salesman was probably right. This R2 unit now had a damaged motivator, and I was sure the second car we picked would be just as good, if not better.

III.

I've been kidnapped by Elvis-loving G. I. Joe.

Though he hasn't officially confirmed it yet, I'm pretty sure this is my first afterlife counselor. Green is easily six feet tall and almost as wide, looking a bit out of place in our Bandit Trans Am. He's all army, a jolly green giant of a man with biceps thicker than my legs. The only things breaking up the be-all-that-you-can-be motif is the large white Stetson on top of his very tanned head and a pair of gaudy aviator sunglasses.

"You like the hat?" Green asks.

I look at it again and shrug. Hats were never my thing.

"I brought one for you." He points a thumb at the tiny back seat. Sitting on top of a large pile of guns is another Stetson. "Go ahead, try it on."

"No thanks," I say. I'm now more concerned about the arsenal on the back seat of the car.

"Why not? Stetsons are the dog's bollocks."

"The what?"

"Sorry, it's a British thing. I adopted it after spending time with some Brits in Afghanistan. Thought it sounded great. It means, 'really fucking good.'"

I look at the hat again and shrug. "I don't see the point."

Corporal Green stops smiling his big bright smile. The inside of the car gets darker and seems more foreboding suddenly.

"Put on the damn hat, Pringate. Live a little."

I'm not sure how wearing a stupid cowboy hat means I'm "living," especially now since I'm supposed to be dead, but I figure I'll try and stay on Green's good side. I reach back, grab the hat, and put it on.

"You've got it on backward, numbnuts."

I correct the hat. "Happy?"

Green's smile brightens up the car again. He reaches over and drops the sun visor in front of me. "Awesome, take a look. Now we're Stetson buddies."

I look in the mirror. There I am, in a cowboy hat. It actually fits my head which is a relief. It also looks silly, but as I turn my head from left to right, it goes from silly stupid to silly fun. I can't help it, I smile.

"See, told you. Cool, huh?" says Green.

I don't confirm or deny the coolness of my new hat, but I do adjust the brim down a little to give myself a more mysterious cowboy vibe. I probably look like an idiot.

"My name is Corporal Green. Let's get the get-ta-know-ya shit out of the way. I proudly served the United States Marine Corps. I did two tours in Afghanistan, and another two in Iraq, until a roadside bomb popped my clogs and sent me straight to God's Almighty Heaven. Originally from Bradford, Ohio. Wasn't much for schoolin' and I love The King."

Corporal Green stabs the power button on the car stereo with his muscular finger. *All Shook Up* by Elvis Presley erupts from the car's speakers. My guess is, "popped clogs," is another British thing.

"And you're my first counselor?" I ask.

"What?"

I turn the stereo off. "And you're my first counselor?"

"Affirmative."

I don't pay attention to where we are going. We leave Anaheim, and it looks like we are eastbound on the 91 freeway, which is also devoid of traffic just like the city. It's just us and the road.

"Where are we going?" I ask.

"We're getting away from the city. We need some time to train before Eugene finds you again."

"Train?"

"Yes, sir. The guns are back there. We're going to squeeze off a few rounds. Get you comfortable with the equipment."

Here we go again with the guns, first at the police station and now here. Welcome to the afterlife, sponsored by the National Rifle Association. "I don't get it. I thought I was supposed to be proving something here. 'Living' or some such bullshit. How does being a gun-toting cowboy do that?" I take off the Stetson and throw it back over the arsenal behind me.

I need a drink. My shoulders are bunched up around my ears, twisted and uncomfortable. The back of my neck aches with stress.

"Pringate, chill out, man. The guns aren't important. Defending yourself from that Eugene fella is. If all this came down to a drinking competition I'm sure you'd win, but it won't, and you need to get with the program."

Oh nice, I'm being judged. I think about how ridiculous that is—of course I'm being judged. I'm dead and stuck in some bullshit pearly gate ultimate challenge.

"Fine. So, where are we going?"

"I know a place off the beaten track where we shouldn't be bothered by anyone for a while."

I look around again. We are just a few miles away from the 15 freeway, and we are still the only car on the road.

"Can we stop here? Where is everyone?"

"This theater was created for you, Pringate. People are added as needed. Do you like the car?"

He doesn't answer my first question, but I did wonder about the Trans Am.

"It's the Bandit's Trans Am. Of course, I do. It's a class-ic. Why is it here?"

"Taylor. She knows you like movies and cars, so she's incorporating that into this game. Anything to inspire that sorry-ass soul of yours."

I think back again to the Venn diagram and the separate circle disconnected from Heaven, Hell, and the Earth as I once knew it. It's hard to keep the fact I'm dead straight in my head when everything around me looks so real. I feel real too, yet here I am, sitting in Sally Field's seat.

"Is my ex-wife Donna here?" I ask.

"Is she dead?" asks Corporal Green.

"I don't think so."

"Then no, she's not here, she's with the living, on Earth. This is an exact copy of where you lived. It's like the universe snapped a big old picture of your little life as you died. She probably had living quarters around here someplace. We can visit after your training if you like. Your afterlife consultant, Taylor, will likely know where she lives."

That sounds like a good way forward, and I want to do that instead of this annoying weapons training. All this cowboy stuff gives me butterflies.

If Donna is responsible for my death, there might be some evidence in her apartment. I'm not sure what I'd do if I found anything incriminating, but at least I'd know one way or another. If she is guilty of my murder, knowing that she'll spend the rest of eternity in a foul mood in Hell, gives me some pleasure.

Corporal Green interrupts my train of thought with an awful Elvis impersonation. "So, this Donna chick. A real, Heartbreak Hotel, oh-huh-huh?"

IV.

I met Donna at our company Christmas party, our mandatory pilgrimage to Monty's Indian Restaurant just down the road from our office. The CEO of our company, Mr. Singh, who was originally from India, liked curry so much we were forced to celebrate the silly season with kormas, chicken tikka masala, tandooris, and all the naan bread we could eat. No open bar, though, which was a shame, but that didn't stop me. What were Christmas bonuses for anyway?

As we were leaving the office to head over to the restaurant, Donna, a visiting sales rep from a local computer memory manufacturer, caught Mr. Singh's eye and was invited along. I couldn't blame him, even though he was a married man. Donna looked good in her navy-blue suit jacket and straight-leg pants. It was your standard issue tech-saleswoman outfit, mostly business professional, but designed to reveal enough to fluster geeky male I.T. managers into handing over large checks for equipment they didn't need. The outfit practically demanded, "Impress me with your checkbook, big boy!"

From what I'd overheard, she was promised a "tasty cultural experience." Something told me that had very little to do with papadums.

Despite Mr. Singh's apparent intentions, Donna seemed quite happy to tag along and get a ride to Monty's in his cherished Mercedes-Maybach. Not that I could blame her either. Mr. Singh may have been roughly thirty years older than Donna, and a little round in the middle, but he was a distinguished, friendly man who had aged well. He treated his staff with respect and was generous with his cheapness— lots of small gestures, like boxes of almost-out-of-date doughnuts or bagels from one of his businesses, that kind of thing.

Monty's wanted to be an Indian restaurant, but its Ruby's Diner origins were painfully obvious. No amount of fake Roman pillars and TV's playing Bollywood movies was going to hide that. Its poorly painted vistas of idyllic Indian country settings (probably created by Mr. Singh's kids—he owned the restaurant, of course) and an almost religious obsession with fake gold fixtures, didn't mesh well with the diner-esque red booths and napkin dispensers that looked like tiny jukeboxes.

The restaurant's staff was Indian (more of Mr. Singh's relatives forced into the family business, no doubt) and clearly wanted to be anywhere else. Each wore a scowl and said very little we could actually hear. Communication between the staff was mostly done with subtle gestures. A glare, an eyebrow lowered, a side glance to a customer's table. It all hinted at the imminent approach of a small revolution inside Monty's. Every single one of them looked ready to explode the next time someone asked about the Bollywood movies, or which part of India they were from. Judging by how un-Indian the staff's accents sounded when they did speak, I assumed the answer to that last question was something like, "I'm from Irvine, you dipshit!"

Our Indian Christmas parties followed a strict schedule. Mr. Singh would let us out of the office at 2 p.m., and we would get to the restaurant around 2:15 p.m. As we walked into the restaurant, one of Mr. Singh's offspring would hand out raffle tickets and then grumpily point to a table of prizes. Each prize would have a small white plastic cup in front of it. Everything from store gift cards to coffee machines were up for grabs. The grand prize was always a forty-two-inch high-definition television.

All sourced from our company website, as usual.

We'd put our tickets into the cups in front of the prizes we wanted to win. I threw all the tickets I had into the cup in front of a Keurig coffee machine. That increased my chances of winning, and it was the only thing I wanted. This also meant I didn't have to check tickets all afternoon. I found this game stressful and the thought of winning made me nervous. I'd have to get up in front of everyone to accept my prize. I suppose I could have thrown away my tickets and not taken part, but I really wanted that coffee machine. A few beers would make everything a little easier to deal with.

The food would already be arranged as a buffet option at the far end of the restaurant, and by 2:45 p.m. we would all have filed past, selected our food and then found a table or a booth. At 3 p.m., Mr. Singh would start shouting out numbers and handing out the prizes.

This always, and somehow only, took exactly two hours. And in all the years at the company, I never won a damn thing. One year, I went all in on a stupid soda machine. I didn't even want it, it was the most unpopular gift there. I saw that only one other person had put in a single ticket, and I still lost.

Mr. Singh was in a grumpy mood on account of his wife having made a rare appearance at our holiday event. I guessed she wanted to be seen with her husband and the common folk. She arrived in a blaze of color, wearing a blue and yellow kurti tunic and a shit ton of gold jewelry. She was ready to play the part of game show hostess handing out prizes to the poor masses, with a fake look of pity on her overly made-up face as she tried to read and understand the bemused expressions we were all making.

As a result of Mrs. Singh's arrival, Donna had been forced to sit with the workforce, and since the place was full—and I wasn't welcome in any of the office cliques— she ended up sitting across from me in a booth near the back of the restaurant.

Not that she saw me at all. Her smartphone was way more interesting, apparently.

While I had created a mountain of rice and chicken korma on my plate and was washing it all down with Elephant Beer paid for out of my own pocket, she nibbled on a single piece of veggie bajji. The Bollywood movies played on.

"You don't like Indian food?" I asked.

She seemed surprised I was there. "Er, no, not really." She looked over my shoulder and waved at Mr. Singh. She was angling to escape, but Mr. Singh and his table of prizes were too close to the main entrance. I turned and saw the old Indian give Donna an apologetic look. He was about to wave back, but was nudged back into action by his wife.

"You could leave. He won't do anything weird with his wife here," I said.

"That's okay. I'd rather slip away unnoticed."

Mr. Singh read another number out, and another nonplussed member of the call center walked up to claim their prize. My chance at the Keurig had come and gone. Damn it.

"We'll be finished at five. Guaranteed. You'll be able to escape then," I said.

Donna focused on me again and smiled. I chose to believe she was impressed that I knew what she was thinking. She checked the time on her phone. "Okay, great. Not long to go then. Mr. Singh does this every year?"

"Yup. Three hours of curry and a raffle. It's okay though, Mr. Singh is cool."

"How long have you worked for the company?"

"Oh, nearly twenty-two years." Then I lied. "I manage the call center."

"Really. That's a long time. Mr. Singh must like you."

I actually didn't think Mr. Singh knew I existed. "Oh yeah, we go way back."

"He certainly seems to do well for himself, and his wife. With all that gold on her face, she looks like a fucking Christmas tree."

I grabbed a paper napkin from my mini tabletop jukebox and coughed up a piece of korma. I tried to stop laughing and apologize for spitting food at the same time.

"You okay?"

I nodded.

Donna focused her attention back to her phone, and just like that, our brief connection seemed to be over. I was impressed with myself that I lasted as long as I did. Thank you, Elephant Beer. Was I attracted to Donna? Absolutely. Did I think I stood a chance with her? Of course not.

At almost 5 p.m., everyone except me was on the edge of their seats as Mr. Singh read out the numbers for the high-definition TV, the only prize anyone cared about. Even Donna seemed curious about the outcome and put down her phone.

Mr. Singh read out the numbers nice and slow for maximum effect. "Three. Five."

Multiple groans around the room signaled the disappointment of non-three-five people.

"Seven."

More groans, and losing tickets found the floor. As far as I could tell there were five people left in the running. They were the only ones still jumping around in their seats excitedly clutching their tickets.

"Eight."

Two more tickets perished violently. We had three contestants left and one number. Mr. Singh looked around the room one more time and pretended to have trouble reading the last digit.

"Six!"

The last three hopefuls responded. "Fuck!" "Shit!" "Whoo-hoo!"

Mr. Whoo-hoo was Carl, and he worked in the call center in the cubicle next to mine. I wouldn't say we were friends, but we had had the occasional conversation between irate customer calls.

Carl leaped out of his booth and jogged up to Mr. Singh. The ticket was deemed legitimate, and everyone begrudgingly gave Carl a round of applause.

Time for one last Elephant Beer before my trip to the liquor store.

A jubilant Carl crash-landed in our booth next to me. He'd had a few beers of his own. "Hi, buddy!" He hugged me. We weren't buddies, and now I was hoping he wouldn't trip up my lie about running the call center, because Carl did.

"Congratulations," said Donna.

Carl stared at Donna for a couple of seconds, and then at me. A look of utter bewilderment on his face. His simple brain likely putting two and two together and got a love connection. I didn't want to correct him.

With his arm around my shoulders, he cut Donna off before she could clarify that we were not, in fact, an item. "You see this guy? This guy is awesome." He shook me to confirm my awesomeness. I had picked up a wingman.

Donna played along. "Really? How so?"

I must admit, I was curious as to what made me awesome in Carl's eyes. As far as I could remember we'd only talked about movies and cars.

"The Sin Pack. That's 'how so.'"

Oh, and there was that.

"My girl," Carl continued. "My girl, Stephanie. She gets this thick envelope from her parents full of newspaper clippings about living in sin. She had told them we were moving in together, pre-marriage, you understand?"

Donna nodded.

"Well, I'm not religious. I say do whatever makes you happy. As long as you're not hurting anyone. Why not? Right?"

"Right," Donna said. I wasn't sure if she actually agreed or was just placating Carl so that he would get through his story as quickly as possible.

"But this pissed me off. Fucking Sin Pack. Stephanie was upset and didn't want to move in with me anymore."

"So how did—" Donna gestured at me.

"George," I said.

"How did George help?"

Yup, she wanted Carl's story to end. Her phone was packed away, and somehow, she had managed to move to the end of the booth without me noticing. She was ready to go.

Carl continued. "So, I'm talking to George about it, and he says 'talk to a priest.'" Carl made the universally understood gesture of a mind blown away. "I was like, what? And he says, 'you need a higher power, go talk to someone her parents won't feel comfortable arguing with.'"

"And what happened next?" Donna asked.

"Well, Stephanie and I were hardly regular visitors to the church, and I felt weird about tracking down someone and begging them to tell Stephanie's parents what they can do with their Sin Pack. They'd probably agree with Stephanie's parents anyway. That's where this guy," Carl squeezes me again, "this guy offers to get ordained! You can do that shit online these days. We figured, he could first pretend to be a priest, and if that didn't work, threaten to marry us. If they called his bluff, he'd take the course and pronounce us man and wife."

Donna turned to face me and tilted her head slightly. Had I impressed her in some small way? Carl suddenly seemed to remember he had a drink and took a slug. "Anyway. Long story short. George has a couple of beers for luck and calls Stephanie's parents. He gives himself some big holy sounding title and then feeds them some crap about life being all about love and charity. When they started to question him, he offered to marry us. They didn't like that at all."

"So, did Stephanie's parents do anything else after that?" asked Donna. She seemed genuinely interested in the story now.

"We're moving in together in a couple of weeks."

Carl pulled me close and aggressively kissed my temple. "Thank you, buddy. You're a freaking genius."

Carl grabbed his drink and left us. He marched his happy self up to the prize stand, grabbed his television, and left the restaurant. I didn't talk to Carl much after the Sin Pack incident. The truth was, I went to this extreme to make a friend, but I ended up outliving my usefulness. We met up a couple of times for drinks, but his excitement about a guy's night out seemed disingenuous and wouldn't last past three drinks. This always pissed me off, which probably showed, and then Carl started to make excuses.

I couldn't see Mr. Singh or his wife. The way out was clear. I pointed at the exit. "I think you can make your escape now."

Donna slid back into our booth.

"I think I'll stay awhile longer." She pointed at my beer. "Is that any good?"

"Elephant Beer? It's the best. Can I get you one?"

"Sure, that'll be great."

Thank you, Elephant Beer. Thank. You.

V.

Corporal Green exits the 15 freeway onto a dirt track; an old faded sign tells me it's called Johnson Road. He doesn't ease up on the throttle, and the Trans Am bounces and skids over the path, kicking up dirt and stones that tickle the car's undercarriage. The guns piled on the backseat slide around, and some fall onto the floor, along with my Stetson.

"So, it sounds like this Donna chick liked to play the angles," he says.

"How would you know?"

Green throws up a hand and shrugs. "Hey, we're working with your memories here. When your ex-wife couldn't connect with that Indian fella, she tried you on for size. Maybe she saw something in you?"

"She said I had a spark."

"A spark, huh?"

Johnson Road becomes a proper tarmac road when it crosses Stoddard Wells Road. The town of Victorville, the closest thing we have to civilization, is six minutes behind us and ahead, not much. On our right, I can see a huge, plain white building, probably a distribution point for a big retailer. Like everything else on our road trip, it seems abandoned. I can't see any cars in the parking lot or any delivery trucks.

"She married me, didn't she? That's got to mean something," I say.

"Bollocks. I'd say she fucked up. She wasn't getting any younger and was clearly desperate."

Green glances at me over his sunglasses like he's expecting a reaction. I think his last comment was mean-spirited, but as he glares at me, I can't be sure. Or I am sure, but I don't want to call him on it. I play the line back a couple of times in my mind. *That was a shitty thing to say, right?* I hardly know the guy, but it seems out of character. *Maybe he meant something else?* I don't know how to respond and look away. *File it away, I'll think about it later.*

"Jesus Christ, Pringate! You're going to let me get away with that?"

"It's okay, don't worry about it."

"No, it's not okay, Pringate. You've got to stand up for yourself. You're the kid who sits at the back of the class, or the guy at parties who spends all his time with the family pet or gets hammered before talking to anyone."

"So? So what?"

"That's not living, Pringate."

Corporal Green takes a hard right as we pass the distribution center and the next sign I see says we're close to Apple Valley Airport.

"It was my life, wasn't it?" I ask.

"Sure. But you're also here with me now. I'm sure Taylor told you at your orientation. Thinking, feeling life is incredibly rare in the universe."

"Yeah, yeah, yeah, and it's not to be wasted."

"Exactly. Going to Heaven or Hell, or whatever you want to call those places, isn't only about not being a crap person. It's about how you use your time while you're alive."

"So, a bad person can go to Heaven?"

"No. If you're an asshole, you're going down. It's where you belong. But at least you'll belong somewhere. Something's been holding you back, Pringate, and you'd better figure out what before that wanker Eugene gets hold of you."

We approach the airport and Green steers our car onto the runway and skids to a halt. I don't see any people, cars, or planes anywhere. It's just us and a few unremarkable buildings. I think on his last comment about belonging, and I don't like it. Belonging probably means with other people in a group. The very idea makes me nervous, and I crave a beer. I'd be happier out here in the desert by myself. If it were possible to not "belong" somewhere, then this nowhere would work just fine for me.

I get out of the car first. It's so quiet; not even a breeze disturbs the peace. It's notable because being from Orange County, I'm conditioned for the constant noise. The rush of cars on the freeway, police sirens, and planes overhead. An industrial soundtrack we all contribute to.

The silence is broken when Corporal Green gets out of the car.

He grabs my Stetson and tosses it to me. "Here, put this back on. It'll keep the sun out of your eyes while we train."

I put the hat on again, the right way this time. It must be midday as the hot sun is blazing directly above us. My entire body starts to sweat. I don't know why we can't train indoors; it's not like there's anyone around to complain. Those buildings probably have plenty of space and air conditioning. The Denny's had electricity, so I'm assuming the power grid works every-where we go.

Green opens the trunk and grabs a large canvas duffel bag. "Pick some hardware off the back seat, will ya?"

I flip the passenger seat forward and look at the arsenal available to me carpeting the entire back end of the car. I see pistols, shotguns, and what might be automatic rifles. I'm not an expert on such things and never wanted to be.

In amongst the hardware I see a belt equipped with two holsters. Each holster holds a gun straight out of a classic western movie. They have white—I'm guessing ivory— handles connected to well-polished steel bodies. I take a closer look and see that the handles have been beautifully carved with a bald eagle design. They seem too pretty to be practical.

I take the pretty guns with their belt and extra ammunition. I also pick up a shotgun. While making my selection,

I notice a bag buried behind the front passenger seat. I open it to find a bunch of different-sized white boxes inside. Probably more ammunition. I take the bag and throw it over my shoulder.

I walk over to Green, who is on the other side of the runway near a wire fence. On every support post, I see a piece of fruit stuck to the top: oranges, cantaloupe, and watermelons.

"Let's see what you picked out," he says.

Green grabs the shotgun and takes the bag of ammunition. "Those look pretty," referring to the holstered guns I'm carrying. "Why don't you put that on. Be a proper cowboy."

I know the guns are probably real, or at the very least, real in this version of the afterlife. But I still feel like a child getting ready for Halloween when I strap the gun belt on. The leather belt, extra ammunition, and guns feel clunky and heavy against my hips. I keep having to haul them upwards as I try to buckle the belt tightly around my waist. It takes me a couple of attempts to finally get it right, both guns level with each other on my hips. I take one of the guns out of the holster.

"What are these?" I ask.

Green takes a closer look. "Those are Colt Single Action Army 45s. You've probably seen a few westerns in your time. Maybe you saw The King in Charro or Flaming Star?"

"No, sorry. Not an Elvis fan. Terrible actor. I've watched a few Clint Eastwood and John Wayne movies. *Unforgiven*, *True Grit*. Those were good."

Green smiles at me but holds it just long enough to tell me it's not really a smile. I think I may have just insulted his own personal Jesus.

"I'll pretend I didn't hear you say that, Pringate."

He snatches the Colt out of my hand and after a couple of fancy twirls, it lands back in my holster. "Can Eastwood or Wayne play the guitar?"

I should have known better than to insult Elvis in front of a mega-fan.

"No, I don't think so."

"Can Eastwood and Wayne sing?"

"Probably not well."

I could argue that these were meaningless skills next to actual acting, for a movie star, but I'm not going to push my luck.

"Then shut the fuck up, Pringate. Here." Green hands me the shotgun and then drags me by the shoulder in front of a large watermelon stuck on a fence pole about forty feet away. "There you go, Eastwood, shoot the bloody watermelon."

I look at the shotgun in my hands. The main part of the gun is black, and the handle, or whatever it's called, is made of wood. There's another wooden section further down. From what I've seen in the movies, this is the bit you pull back to chamber a new cartridge. I do that. I hear the mechanism inside click twice. I look at Green to confirm I did it right. He's giving me nothing.

Then the gun goes off. If I was aiming at the sky, then kudos to me—target acquired and destroyed. I drop the gun and jump backward.

"What the sweet hell are you doing, Pringate?" shouts Corporal Green.

"I don't know; it just went off."

Green picks up the shotgun and inspects it; he's focused on the gun but still seems distracted.

"I mean, have you ever met The King?" asks Green.

Oh jeez, what have I done? "No. Look, I—"

"Well, I have. He's sitting in God's playground right now making sweet music. He served in the United States Army, and he's a fucking rock legend. That's a life well lived, Pringate. What did you ever do?"

"Look, I'm sorry I said Elvis was a bad actor, okay?"

Corporal Green hands me the shotgun and shrugs as though trying to pretend my words haven't cut him deeply. *Who would have thought this big army dude could be such a snowflake about a musician?*

"You can apologize to the Man yourself if you ever stop being a lifeless screw up."

I feel my relationship with Green has taken a dark turn and may never recover. He has a point, however. What have I done? Where do I get off criticizing an American legend? Love him or hate him, Elvis lived a full life. His music still entertains millions of people around the world; his sexually charged performances upset the pious. I wonder how they'd feel now if they knew he was still gyrating to adoring fans in Heaven. I'm maybe starting to understand what is expected of me with all this afterlife nonsense. Why would Heaven want you if you hadn't used your time on Earth to do anything meaningful? If all you did was grow old and die, forgotten, without at least trying to make your mark. Without leaving something behind that said "George Pringate was here."

There are those butterflies again, that energy that comes from nowhere I can understand and muddies my thinking. *Who said you had to do anything with your life? You're not Elvis. Your creative efforts are worthless.* Doesn't it seem like famous people were special even before they hit it big? Tom Hanks was Tom Hanks before he became Tom Hanks, right? Friends of superstars in interviews always claim they knew Mr. or Ms. Big Shot Movie Star was going to make it big. Sure, they worked for their place, but they always claim they were lucky and in the right place at the right time. Was it destiny? Were all the elements in Meryl Streep's life designed to click at just the right moments to ensure her record number of Oscar nominations? Was I destined for a life on the phone in a call center? Were all those unfinished screenplays I had at home as worthless as I thought they were?

I take the shotgun and chamber another round. *Click click.* Maybe if I shoot this stupid watermelon, Corporal Elvis-nut will be happy, and we can go and get a beer. I know I'm being hunted, but there has to be a place we can go where it is safe for me to tune out for a while. I need a break from the argument in the back of my mind. It's getting loud and hard to ignore.

I level the shotgun and point it in the general direction of the watermelon. Then I hear a car honk its horn. A pathetic sound only a small car makes.

Coming into focus through the hot desert air radiating from the runway tarmac, I see a beat-up VW Beetle. From a distance, it looks like one of my favorite cars growing up, but when it gets close enough to see clearly, it most certainly isn't the Love Bug from all those Disney movies I enjoyed. The car is more rust white than pearl, and the stripes, red, white, and blue, look like they have been recently painted on with a brush. The '53' decal is all wrong too. It reads '52.' This isn't the automobile that got me interested in cars. This is a child's nightmare.

I put the gun down on the ground and start to walk toward the car. I can't help it; I'm curious.

I only get a couple of feet before Corporal Green stops me.

"What the hell are you doing, Pringate?"

"I'm going to take a closer look. That paintwork is all wrong."

"Yeah, and why would someone drive out to meet us in the desert with a car like that? Oh, I don't know, maybe someone who is looking for you? Trying to kill you maybe?"

I didn't think of that. I am such an idiot.

"Hello!" We are interrupted by the Beetle's driver, Eugene. He and his car are stopped about fifty feet away. "You know, you can't hide from me, Pringate. I'm drawn to you like a fly on shit."

A lovely image.

Corporal Green reaches out and grabs the back of my shirt. "We've got to go, Pringate. This is a trick, a temptation. If you go over there, it's over for you."

"But he's not trying to shoot us," I say.

"He doesn't have to. He'll take you dead, or alive if you're willing. He'd love to rub that in Taylor's face."

Eugene continues, "Do you like the car? One of your childhood favorites if I'm not mistaken."

"I don't think so," I reply.

"Really?" Eugene eyes the car.

"Not even close."

Green says, "You got the number wrong, numbnuts!"

"Really?" Eugene shrugs. He has the appearance of a man who doesn't give a shit. "Well, fuck it."

Eugene lifts the hood and pulls out a medium-sized cooler. He sets it on the ground and opens it up. Even from this distance, I can hear his hands push past ice cubes. He produces two bottles of beer. "Look, George, I'm sorry about all that business at the police station. I hadn't finished my research. It seems you and I have quite a bit in common."

He holds up the beer, and I finally notice what he's wearing. He still looks like an ashtray with arms and legs, but he'd managed to brighten things up with a red and gold pineapple print shirt, khaki shorts, flip-flops, and a straw hat.

"What do you say, George? You and me, a few cold brews. I've got a couple of chairs in the back. We can drink, drive this piece of shit car into the ground and watch the sunset."

I know what part of this universe this Eugene dude is from, and on some level, I understand that nothing good would come from his offer. But isn't that always the way before a good drink? You know there's a price to pay, but you polish off that twelve-pack anyway. Each time you swear you'll never drink again, but a few days later there you are with a can in your hand. You black out, wake up in a strange place, but after a couple of days, all is forgiven. The time between sessions gets shorter until you're justifying the "hair of the dog" drink in the morning, and before you know it, the days you don't drink are few and far between. God, I want to sit with Eugene and help him empty that cooler. My mouth feels dry, and he has just what I need. Fuck it, and fuck this stupid game.

No. I had been there before. I had traveled that path and hated how wrong it felt. I had managed this. *How many days has it been since your last drink?* No, we're not doing it. *It's got to be a week; you're due, it's okay.* No, it's not! This guy is going to send me to Hell! *So? They'll at least have beer there.*

Corporal Green steps up behind me and whispers in my ear. "Take a step back, Pringate."

My hands turn into fists. The argument rages.

Green's voice helps me focus. "Take one step back with me. Just one."

He gently pulls at my shirt, and I take a step back.

"Now, another."

We take another step back. I keep my eyes on Eugene, and he doesn't look happy.

"Hey, where are you going? Are you leaving? After I brought the beer and drove this crappy little car out here?"

I take another step back with Green, and then another. We are almost back to the Trans Am.

Eugene turns back to his cooler. "Maybe this will convince you to stay."

He pulls a small pistol out of the ice and starts shooting at us.

Green returns fire with the shotgun. He misses Eugene but puts a big hole in the Beetle's hood. We reach the Trans Am and use it for cover.

"Okay, here's your moment, Pringate. Take one of those 45s and blow that fucker's head off!"

Bullets ricochet off the hood and hit the tires on the other side of the car.

"NOW, PRINGATE!"

I can't think and press my hands against my ears. Green grabs one of my hands and shouts at me again.

"Time to step up, Pringate. Grab life by the balls and stand up for yourself."

I can't do it. *Just shoot the gun.* I think I have to want to shoot the gun. *You don't want to?* I want to run away.

Corporal Green stands up and marches around the car toward Eugene, firing the shotgun to a steady rhythm. Click click, BANG, click click, BANG.

I hear someone cry out in agony. I look over the hood of the car and see Eugene on the ground rolling around. The bottom half of his left leg and his right elbow have been vaporized. Blood gushes out of his arm and leg, leaving dark, impressionistic designs on the tarmac.

Corporal Green is on the ground, face down, a pool of blood forming under his head. Seeing him there sends a chill down my spine. Is he gone for good? He shot Eugene before, and that asshole recovered. I call out, "Corporal Green!"

"God damn that Elvis-loving freak! That's for shooting me through the door," says Eugene. "Shit this hurts."

Eugene rolls over to his severed arm. It's still holding his gun. He grabs the gun with the hand he has left. "Just stay put, you piece of shit. I'll be there in a minute. Fuck this is painful. Never lost this many limbs before."

I hide behind the car again. I hear Eugene drag his body over the tarmac; each effort is punctuated by the sound of his gun scraping against the runway.

I am a few hundred feet from the nearest building. Maybe if I keep the Trans Am between myself and Eugene, I can make it over there.

The sound of Eugene's body crawling over the ground ceases.

I run. The guns on my hip make it hard though, so I take them off and let them fall to the ground. I run toward the nearest building, bullets whizzing by me, striking the dirt by the runway.

I'm not sure where I'm going. After reaching the building, I can see how far the 15 freeway is. With no wheels available, I'm on foot for the time being. My new body seems up for a run though, so I figure it won't be long before I get back to Victorville. From there, I'm not sure. I don't know how all this works. Do I get another counselor? Did I already fail my test? Has Eugene won?

Chapter 3: Focus

I.

After running for approximately ten minutes, I get back to the 15 freeway. My new body tells me I have plenty more energy in the tank, so I keep heading south, back toward Victorville. I don't know what I'm going to do when I get there, but this plan is better than waiting around for Eugene to surprise me like some kind of last-act-of-the-movie Terminator. Sure, it looks incapacitated and then, BAM! He boots up and crawls after you again.

I heard Eugene say he hadn't lost "this many limbs before." So there's a good chance he's already recovered. Do they grow back like Deadpool's? Or maybe they reappear in a flash of light? In any case, I run alongside the freeway as there are more options for cover. If I hear Eugene's *Herbie* knockoff rolling down the road, I can use a bush or road sign to hide behind. It's better than no plan at all.

I hope there's a bar open somewhere in Victorville. Left to my own devices as I am, the image of me hidden away in some dank, dark hole with a beer looks appealing. If no one is around, I can help myself. It might be a good hiding place too. A win-win.

I think about Corporal Green, dead on the tarmac. I guess I let him down. He was only trying to help, after all. I tell myself he isn't actually dead since he technically already was. He's probably sitting with his hero Elvis talking about how much of a loser I am. I wonder if he'll pass on that "bad actor" comment? If I do what I'm supposed to do here, whatever that is, I may have to explain myself to The King. That would be surreal.

I hear a car approach from behind. It's still about a mile away, but from what I can make out it's not the bug. I hide behind a bush at the side of the road and wait for the car to pass.

A red Plymouth Fury arrives and stops near my position. It has to be the 1958 model used in the movie *Christine*. Talk about a car the devil's servant would drive. I tuck myself in tighter against my cover, trying to be small and easy to miss.

"Mr. Pringate!" shouts Taylor, my Transition Consultant. *Shit.*

There she is, still rocking her pink catsuit, standing by the side of the road, waving.

"Get in the damn car," she says.

I climb up the side of the freeway. Taylor throws me the keys to the car. "You drive."

Somewhat relieved that Eugene has not tracked me down and excited I get to drive the Plymouth, I walk around to the driver's side while Taylor lowers herself onto the back seat.

The Plymouth is in pristine condition. Double barrel front headlamps, a big, aggressive grill, and polished chrome. It's a massive work of art. I've always loved this car. I love this era of car design. Its gross inefficiencies are only matched by the gorgeous design details: the whitewall tires, massive rear fenders, and little fins sticking out of the metalwork right above the front headlights.

"Stop admiring the car, Pringate. It isn't going to take long before Eugene gets back into this game," yells Taylor from her open window.

I open up the driver's side door and slide onto the big, sofa-like seat.

"Let's go. Head back to Anaheim. I have the address of your ex-wife," says Taylor.

I whip my head around on hearing this, but I'm distracted by the little girl who sits next to my Transition Consultant. "You do? —who is that?"

The little girl, who looks to be around four or five years old, is dressed in blue jeans and a Dora the Explorer T-shirt. A mostly pink T-shirt that matches the mostly pink, Dora-themed backpack sitting next to her. She doesn't look up from the handheld Nintendo game console she's playing. She probably isn't even able to hear us through the big, noise-canceling headphones covering her ears.

"This is Christine, just like the car we're in," says Taylor.

I let out a short laugh. "Really? Christine? You know why this car is famous, right?"

"What? I thought it was cute that one of your favorite cars had that name."

"Cute? You obviously haven't read the Stephen King book or seen the movie. Tell me, is little Christine here a murderous, possessed killing machine too?"

"Well of course not. I guess I should have researched this a little more. It's hardly important."

Taylor taps Christine on the shoulder to get her attention. Christine pushes back one of her headphones.

Briefly, I hear the sound of Christine's game playing before she pauses it.

"Christine, this is Mr. Pringate."

I smile like a dork as Christine looks me over. Eventually, she speaks. "Hi, Mr. Pringate."

I feel like I have been judged and found wanting. I know, I'll ask her about her game, that'll win me some brownie-points.

She ignores my question and turns to Taylor. "Why am I here?"

Taylor looks both a little embarrassed and irritated. "I told you, you're here to help Mr. Pringate."

"But why do I have to be five years old? I haven't been into Dora in a decade."

It was an odd question to be sure, and it got me wondering about a few things. Did you get to pick your age when you headed afterlife-way? Is it chosen for you? Maybe the universe looks at your entire life history and picks when you peaked? I'm not sure when that would be for me, but if I could keep the body I'm currently in, that would be fine.

"You're five because this is the age you died," Taylor says, rather bluntly I might add, with the clear intention to stop Christine's questions; it works too. Christine gives Taylor a look that would make Hitler uneasy, and then slides her headphones back on and resumes her game.

"Pringate, let's get this show on the road. Drive on, please."

I start the car and shift it into drive. We slowly crawl back onto the freeway and pick up speed. The old Plymouth purrs like a happy, fat cat.

"So, what's her story?" I ask Taylor.

"Christine is your next counselor."

Somehow, this news is hardly surprising to me. Of course she's a counselor. Why not? This universe-adjacent sandbox is just full of weirdness. "Really? And what is she going to teach me? Advanced hand-to-hand combat? Or maybe how to tantrum Eugene to death?"

"You be nice, Pringate. You know, I haven't seen any progress in you yet."

There's Corporal Green again, on the floor. Dying to give me a chance and I run away.

Taylor continues. "Christine here is tougher than she looks, and she's here to help your sorry ass. You have no idea what she's been through."

I am curious, but not sure I want to know how someone so young ended up here.

"It seems a shame she's here. She died when she was five?"

"That's right."

I turn the rearview mirror to get another look at Christine with Taylor. She's pretty, with pale skin and long mouse-brown hair, but seems hardened somehow. Maybe she's just concentrating on her game, but her face suggests wisdom beyond her outward appearance. I get the sense this girl has known disappointment on a tragic scale. That's my limited sense of it anyhow. Something about the vibe I'm getting seems familiar. It's going to be hard to remember she is older.

"How did she, you know?"

Taylor sighs. "Car accident. She wasn't wearing her seatbelt." Taylor brushes Christine's hair behind her ear. Christine pushes Taylor's hand away, and her eyes don't move from her game console.

I'm sorry I asked.

"But that's not important right now. We need to talk about you," says Taylor.

I put my foot down on the accelerator pedal. I have the feeling I'm not going to like this, so I figure I'll try to make the journey as short as possible. It's not like there are any other cars on the road, and I doubt I'll be pulled over for speeding. We'll be back in Anaheim in no time at all.

"Look, I'm sorry about Corporal Green."

"Oh, don't worry about him. He's fine and back enjoying his afterlife. You, on the other hand, might not get one to enjoy if you don't figure this out."

I feel like a school kid getting a dressing down from the headmaster, but then I remember something Eugene said about Taylor. This is maybe a chance to push back and change the subject.

"Hey, what's this I hear about you losing your past clients?"

I see Taylor screw up her face in anger. "Eugene tell you that?"

"Yes."

Taylor sighs. "Well, he's right. Not everyone can be saved. Some people are a lost cause."

That last line has a sharp edge just for me. If this were a tennis match, Taylor just responded to my volley by smashing the ball into my crotch. Game. Set. Match.

She continues. "If you don't make it, then it won't be for the lack of me trying. I hate losing people. It makes me look bad. But believe it or not, the universe has guidelines and expectations. I can't describe to you what'll happen to me if I don't get a win soon, so you had better start concentrating and figure this out. I have put a lot of effort into your salvation. I'm even willing to bend the rules a little if need be. Usually, these cases only require one or two counselors; you're getting three. The maximum allowed."

"Figure what out?" I ask. Why on Earth will no one spell this shit out to me?

"I think you've got to look back further. Investigate your death if you like, but I think you're looking at the wrong moments in your life. Why did you, George Pringate, end up here?"

"I was boring?" I venture.

"Oh please, sure, you were—are—a dull person. But that's not it. There are plenty of boring people in Heaven. But even they at some point in their lives accomplished something. I need you to think about the events in your life that led you to me."

I have no response for Taylor, and I refocus on my driving duties. The only sound inside the car comes from

Christine's little fingers frenetically tapping the game console controls.

It isn't long before we see signs for Anaheim. Taylor leans forward and tells me to take the 91 and exit on Imperial. That is my neighborhood.

If we were heading to my place, we'd take a right on La Palma, but Taylor instructs me to drive on and turn left to hit the connector to Orangethorpe. Well, how about that? Donna moved into an apartment complex less than a mile away from mine. It's incredible we hadn't bumped into each other. She did know all my favorite places, however, so maybe it wasn't so difficult to avoid me. Or spy on me?

We pull into her apartment complex and Taylor guides me to Donna's apartment. I park across the street.

"Okay," says Taylor. "Nobody is around, so you're free to do what you like."

"I can just walk right into her apartment?"

"This whole set up is based on a snapshot I took of your little place in the world, Pringate. Every detail is correct up to the point you passed on. If Donna had anything to do with your death, this is probably the best place to start looking for clues. But don't linger, Pringate, it won't take long for Eugene to find you."

Taylor taps Christine on the shoulder again. Christine turns off her game and removes her headphones. "Is it time?"

"Yes. I've got to go so you stick close to Mr. Pringate here."

To say I'm not on board with the babysitting gig is an understatement. "Seriously, she's not going with you?" I never had kids of my own; never really wanted any. I have no idea what I'm supposed to do with this little human being.

Both Taylor and Christine give me blank stares, likely waiting for me to get with the afterlife program. I grunt,

"Fine, fine." What the heck? Hopefully I'm dealing with a broody teenager inside the five-year-old. At least then she'll be quiet and not bother me.

Taylor kisses Christine on her forehead and then exits the car. I watch her walk down the street behind us. She wears that pink catsuit well. *I'm so easily distracted.*

I get out of the Plymouth and make my way across the street to the large apartment complex and Donna's apartment. It's weird to think everything around me is just an exact snapshot of the world at the moment of my death. That every detail, every piece of paper, or letter, or computer, or toaster, or fridge, or television, is just sitting there waiting for nobody. It might be interesting to visit a few apartments and see what people got up to, but I have a mission of my own.

A cry for help from Christine derails my train of thought. I turn around and find her on the road by the car. It looks like she fell over and hurt herself.

"What happened?" I ask.

"I fell."

"Well, I can see that. Why?"

"I don't know. I tripped. I haven't been five in a while; the muscle control isn't there yet." Christine gets up and dusts herself off. She looks at her palms as small droplets of blood start to form and eventually dry into scabs. She managed to graze her knee too, and rip a hole in her jeans.

II.

My dad was pissed at me, again. I sat in the front passenger seat gingerly touching the bandages over my left eye and the corner of my lip. I winced as our car bounced over a pothole and I jabbed one of my cuts.

"Don't touch the damn bandages!" he shouted at me.

Here I was again, the third miserable car ride home from the hospital in the last year. My dad kept looking over at me, shaking his head in disbelief. He gripped the steering wheel with both hands. For my part, all I could think to do was be small and not move. I wanted to cry, but I fought the feelings inside and tried to keep my face still. I didn't want to risk pulling my stitches out, after all.

"I don't get it, I really don't," Dad said. He loosened his tie and then ran his hand over his short black hair. He'd been called away from work again, apparently interrupting an important meeting. "Why can't you ever stand up for yourself?"

Hours before, I was at school—sixth grade, or as I liked to think of it, Little Hell on Earth. One of the school's bullies (we had a lot; I was their favorite) had found my latest hiding spot and started to chase me around the yard. Once more I was left to fend for myself as other children and teachers ignored the life-or-death drama unfolding right under their noses. This was no game of tag unless of course, your definition of "tag" meant being punched in the face. "You're it, loser!" Pop! Bang! Wallop!

On this occasion, I was lucky to have one of the heavier bullies chasing me. My "running away" experience was paying off as the tubby douchebag struggled to keep up. It wasn't long, however, before we were spotted by the fitter, faster bullies, and my lead started to shrink.

Not that it ultimately mattered. As I rounded the old gym building, looking over my shoulder at my pursuers, I collided with an open window. Pop! Bang! Wallop!

The collision created a half-inch cut right next to my left eye and a small but no less painful gash by my lip. Blood poured down my face and neck, and the bullies, as usual when the blood started to flow, vanished. I got up and staggered toward one of the teachers on patrol in the schoolyard. Shortly afterward, I was rushed to the nurse's office, and then the hospital. Several painful injections and some neat sewing work later, I was ready to go home.

The doctor knew me well. "You again, George. For more stitches, I see."

This wasn't my first rodeo.

Nearly a year ago, after another pointless soul-crushing game of soccer, I was asked (told really, on account I was the worst player on the field) to pack up the equipment. This left me open and alone for attack, and it wasn't long before other players on my team surrounded me.

Their ringleader had decided it would be great fun to have a couple of kids hold me still while they threw a broken piece of glass at me. From what I could see, the glass looked a little like a ninja throwing star, which inspired my tormentors. They took turns throwing it at me, aiming for my bare arms and legs. I struggled, but I couldn't escape. I started to cry. This emboldened the assholes doing impressions of *Ninja Turtles*, trying to open me up.

After a lot of failed attempts, the one who took the name Leonardo finally got the piece of glass to stick in me, right above my right kneecap.

Everyone froze. The dirty piece of glass was stuck there. Maybe half an inch deep. Blood poured down my leg. It actually wasn't that painful, but I cried out anyway. I was let go, and the gang of wannabe ninjas ran away and left me to hobble back to school. As I approached, our gym teacher, who probably wondered what was taking me so long, found me. I was scooped up off the ground and rushed to the nurse's office, and then driven to the hospital.

Four months after that, I was once again on the school field. I had found a good reading spot by a tree. It was wide enough to cast a nice, thick shadow away from the school—a perfect place to hide, read, and wait for my next class. I thought I had managed to escape the schoolyard unnoticed, but I was mistaken.

I had barely opened my latest Spider-Man comic when it was ripped out of my hand. There were only three bullies this time, and they were taller than me. I tried to snatch my comic back, but they held it above my head out of reach. Then the pushing started, and I was pinballed around. Once again, the tears flowed. I felt helpless and couldn't understand why these kids would do this. Why was this satisfying to them? How could this be entertaining?

One final push sent me to the ground, and I felt something stab into my left leg, right above my kneecap.

I got up to find another piece of broken glass stuck in my leg. At least there was going to be some symmetry to my scars. The glass itself was green, probably an old beer bottle. We'd heard that some older kids used the field to drink in. Leaving broken bottles in a middle school's field clearly wasn't a concern for them.

My bullies, on seeing me bleed out once again, ran away. I hobbled back toward the school. I was once again scooped up by a teacher and taken to the nurse's office, and then the hospital for more stitches.

My dad pulled into our driveway. We lived in a pretty decent house in Irvine not far from my school. He took a deep breath and then turned toward me. "Are you sure the hospital called your mother?"

"They said they did."

"They called her first, before me?"

I knew why he was asking and I didn't want to answer. I knew Mom was at home, but the nurse at the hospital said no one answered her calls or responded to the messages she left. Each time I had been at the hospital, the same thing happened. My mom wouldn't answer the phone or say she didn't get the messages. She'd prove it by playing back the blank tape, which meant she erased it, but Dad—giving her the benefit of the doubt—bought her story and replaced the machine. He did this twice. Something told me he wasn't going to buy a third.

"Well?" he pushed.

I nodded my head.

He stabbed the control attached to the visor to open our garage door, and the car lurched inside. Dad got out and marched into the house.

I thought about staying in the car, at least from inside I wouldn't hear them fight this time. Maybe if I just took a minute, their argument would already be over.

I was wrong. Dad had left the front door open, and as soon as I got out of the car, I could hear them yelling at each other. The stairs leading up to my bedroom were close, and I ran inside and closed the door. I had done this plenty of times before. Through the floor, I could still hear them. Dad was shouting at Mom for not going to the hospital to pick me up. Mom complained she was busy. They went into the details on what "busy" was, and I could tell Dad wasn't happy. If only I'd looked where I was going. Why did I have to hit that stupid window?

I heard something crash downstairs. My guess was that Mom threw something because my dad started yelling for her to leave. There was a moment of silence after that. A line had been drawn and crossed and it felt like something big was about to happen.

I sat on the floor and curled up against the wall next to my bed. My parents both stomped upstairs. I couldn't be sure what was happening, but I heard things being thrown around in the walk-in closet in their bedroom. Dresser drawers were opened and slammed shut. Their argument had started up again, but at a lower volume, like they were suddenly worried I could hear them.

Shortly after that only one set of feet stomped back down the stairs—it was Mom. I heard her throw several f-bombs upstairs at my dad before the front door slammed shut.

The house got very quiet after that. I couldn't help it; I started to cry. The salty tears stung when they touched my cut. I felt like I was getting smaller, like a force was pulling me from inside. Each skin cell was connected to my heart via taut rubber bands, wobbling, threatening to snap. I thought I would explode.

I hadn't noticed my dad's footsteps as he approached my room. He knocked on my door and opened it. He spoke so softly like he barely had any energy left. "I'll, er, get dinner ready in a minute. Okay, son?"

I looked up at him; it was hard to see through the tears. I nodded. I think he was in as much pain as I was. If I'd only watched where I was going. If I'd just once stood up to the bullies at school.

My parents got divorced later that year. Occasionally I saw my dad looking over paperwork about it. I could tell he didn't like talking about it with me. But he did tell me my mother couldn't be bothered to fight for custody. It was just going to be me and Dad from now on.

I never saw my mom again.

III.

Am I responsible for Christine now? It is weird to think she's my counselor. I'm not sure what Taylor's game is, but I'm positive Christine will be useless against Eugene.

Having kids of my own was never really a priority for me. I have no good memories of being a child myself. Maybe Christine is just the victim here, forced into this weird game by my desperate Transition Consultant. I don't have time to deal with it. I have plenty to worry about already.

"Listen, Christine. How about you wait in the car while I do what I need to do here?"

Christine looks at the car and then back at me. I can tell she doesn't like the idea. She looks like she's about to cry and she stares at me with her big green eyes. Now I feel like an asshole for even suggesting it. My instincts suggest this is an act as she's suddenly more kid-like than before, but what can I do?

"Okay. Never mind. Let's go."

Christine takes hold of my hand. "Where are we going?" she asks.

I'm not sure how much detail I need to go into. I can hardly tell her I'm going to search my wife's apartment to find out if and why she killed me. "We're going to a friend's house. I think she has something for me to pick up."

"You don't know? She didn't tell you?" asks Christine. *Remember, Pringate, you are talking to a teenager.* What the heck, maybe I should level with her?

"Well, to be honest, she's not home and doesn't know I'm coming."

"Is she here? Will she be mad if you go into her house?"

"No, so I don't think she'll ever know," I say.

Donna's apartment is on the second floor. Christine leads the way up the stairs to the front door. I cup my hands around my eyes and look through the windows into her apartment. There's one window to the left of the door that lets me see her living space and dining area. I see a few envelopes on her small dining table. The other window to the right of her front door reveals her bedroom. Her bed is unmade, which is odd as it's usually the first thing she does after waking up.

It's strange to see signs of Donna's life in this weird afterlife space, on its own outside the normal universe. I know there's no chance Donna is here, but it feels like she'll appear out of nowhere at any moment. I run that scenario through my mind a couple of different ways, and it doesn't go well for me.

I try the door, but of course, it's locked.

"What now?" asks Christine.

"Well, I guess I'll have to break the door down."

"Interesting."

What an odd response, and I'm more convinced than ever that Christine's innocent five-year-old act is exactly that, an act. "You got a problem with me breaking down the door?"

She shakes her head and takes a couple of steps away to give me some room. I eye the door and take a few steps back myself. I've seen a million doors get bashed open on TV. How hard could it be?

I pick a spot and ram it with my shoulder as hard as I can and discover immediately it's actually very difficult to break a door down. My shoulder hurts and I don't want to use it again. I try kicking the door right above the handle. Still nothing, but I think I hear the door frame crack a little. I kick the door again, trying to put all my weight behind my foot. The frame cracks once more. A couple more kicks should do it. I hope.

On the third extra kick, the door swings open. I take a moment to catch my breath, and then I cautiously enter the apartment. I don't know why I'm being so careful and I tell myself to get a grip. *Nobody is here, dumbass.* I know, but— *but nothing, check the fridge.*

I head to the kitchen and open the fridge. *Fuck*. Damn it. *Empty*.

"What the hell?" I slam the fridge door closed.

"What's wrong?" asks Christine.

"Nothing." I lean against the particle board kitchen countertop that's painted to look like gray granite. Christine looks at me, confused. She wouldn't understand. The fact that the fridge was completely empty tells me this isn't an exact copy of Donna's apartment. Taylor probably made sure of that. Before Donna and I lived together, I had visited her old apartment. Her fridge was always a reliable place to go for a beer.

The muscles in my neck and upper back ache, and my shoulder still hurts from when I slammed it into the door. This whole fucking situation can kiss my ass. What am I even going to find here anyway? A note that says "I, Donna, of sound mind and body hereby declare I killed my husband, George"?

It's hard to keep my composure, doubly so now since I don't feel I can vent in front of Christine. A hundred thoughts compete for the top podium spot in my mind. Where was Eugene? *Was there even beer in this stupid afterlife sandbox?* Did Donna murder me? *What will happen to Taylor if I fail?* Do I even care?

"What were you looking for in the fridge?" she asks.

Fine, if she wants to know. "Beer."

"Beer? Why is that important now?"

"You wouldn't understand." *Don't press, kid.*

"Seems stupid to me. You're being hunted, and the only thing on your mind is beer?"

Something about the tone in Christine's voice makes me think she's trying to understand, as opposed to being judgmental. At this moment she's more the naïve five-year-old I see in front of me, and less the teenager that has maybe seen a bit of life.

"Look, Christine, I'm a little stressed out right now, and I've got a lot on my mind. I thought a beer would help. It usually does." *Yeah, that's right it does.*

Christine walks into the kitchen and tugs at my shirt. "Try to concentrate on one thing."

I turn to face her. "What?"

"Focus on one thing."

"What's that going to solve?"

"You said you have a lot on your mind. Try to focus on the most important thing, after the beer of course, and push the rest aside."

Fine, I guess it wouldn't hurt. I focus. One thing. I grab a card from my mental Rolodex and then push the infernal device to the back of my mind. "I want to know if my wife killed me."

Christine doesn't seem surprised. "Okay, so what should we look for?"

That's a great question. "Good question."

"Thank you. Here's another. How would Donna gain from your death?"

Good point. "Great point. Maybe an insurance policy? Our marriage wasn't officially over yet so she could have set something up to pay out after I was gone."

"So, we're looking fooooor?"

I finally click; jeez, I can be slow. "Paperwork!"

"Correct."

"Excellent. Can you check in the bedroom? I'll look through her mail and paperwork in here."

Christine once again acts like a five-year-old. She groans, drops her shoulders, and stomps into Donna's bedroom. I head over to the dining table to check the mail.

Unlike me, Donna is a neat freak. The one-bedroom apartment is small but doesn't feel cluttered. Everything is in its proper place. There is a square dining room table with four chairs neatly arranged around it in the center of the apartment. Next to the table is a sofa and a separate leather chair arranged at ninety degrees to each other around a rectangular rug, in front of the entertainment center. The space between the chair and sofa is filled with a nice square chairside table with two ceramic tile coasters and a very modern, square-shaped zen lamp. I remember her trying to get my place into a similar shape and how much fun I would have moving items a few inches from their designated spot. It used to drive her crazy.

The neatly arranged mail on her table looks like bills, and a couple of them are past due. Even more reason to claim a big insurance payment.

I check the entertainment center next. It's one of those Ikea numbers with multiple compartments and canvas boxes. I pull out a box that's being used to store paperwork, then I sit down on the floor next to it and check out the alphabetized tabs. There it is, under "I" for insurance.

I grab the entire folder and dump it onto the rug. Most of it seems pretty normal to me: car insurance, renters insurance, et-cetera. Donna likes to keep five years of paperwork for each account. I dig through it and eventually find something interesting.

There it is, a life insurance policy.

Reading this stuff was never my forte, but it looks like what I'm after. My name is all over it, next to big numbers and dollar signs. From what I can tell, it looks like Donna stands to earn a tidy $200,000. *Cheeky bitch.*

Christine returns from the bedroom holding a stack of photographs and a small black book. "I didn't find any paper-work, but maybe these are useful? There are a lot of scrapbooks in there too."

I always found it interesting that Donna liked to have physical copies of her photos. She loved other people's pictures too, especially old ones shot on film. She usually did everything on her phone, practically lived inside the device, but in this one area, with pictures and phone numbers, she was old school.

I hold up the insurance policy. "I found it. She did take out a policy on me." I look at Christine, waiting for a response, but get nothing from her. She knows how to play the kindergartner card when she doesn't care about something. "Don't you see, this proves she stood to gain from my death."

Christine shrugs. "Okay, so it's a motive, but doesn't prove anything."

My excitement somewhat dampened, I grab the pictures from Christine's hand. "Well, it's a start."

I cycle through the photos. There's a lot of Donna and me during the happier days of our marriage. As I look at each one, I'm reminded of trips we took together and parties we attended. Better times for the most part, but some of the photos tell a darker story beyond the flash.

I recall how on some occasions I got too drunk and passed out. I'd shut down like an Android with dead batteries, sometimes for up to an hour, then awake to find the party almost over, with everyone avoiding eye contact with me. I'd get the "report" from Donna the next morning and find out how I'd managed to embarrass myself, us. Sometimes I'd get upset and cry, apparently, and sometimes I'd be filled with rage and march back and forth in front of everyone ranting. I never hurt anyone or got into fights, but we stopped getting party invites.

I move past the Memory Lane section of the photos and find something new. Donna, arm in arm with another guy. Some older, yet tall, dark, and handsome asshole with perfect teeth. It stings at first to see her with someone else, but I remind myself why I'm currently sitting on her rug with her insurance paperwork.

I turn the photo over and see a name and a date. "Brad." Oh jeez, he's a Brad? Looks like a fucking Brad. Now I think about that; it doesn't make much sense to me. What's a Brad anyway? *Brads are assholes, of course.* I bet he lingers on the "a" when he introduces himself. "Hi, I'm Braaad." *Ugh, I hate him.* I hate his bleached teeth. *I hate his tan.* I hate that his shirt has a few buttons undone to reveal his hairy chest, and I hate that Donna is exploring his gray chest pubes with her hand. The date tells me this photo was taken a couple of months ago.

I rip the photo in half and then move onto the next one. It's an old picture of my dad and me, a Polaroid selfie I took while we were watching TV together. My dad is not even looking at the camera. As I recall now, however, he had other things on his mind.

IV.

It was just my dad and me after my mother left us, and we quickly settled into our new lives. In order to make things work around his schedule and my school, I would get dropped off early and picked up late, and we'd nearly always visit a drive-thru on the way home. It was kind of awesome, though we both gained a few pounds over the years.

It's weird to think of it this way, but we became great friends. We went to the movies together on the weekends and watched the same TV shows. My dad was a complete geek, and we'd have debates about the silliest things. The

Enterprise from *Star Trek* versus a Star Destroyer from *Star Wars*. General Zod from *Superman* versus Sauron from *The Lord of the Rings*. He seemed quite happy to hang out with me and wasn't interested in dating. Dad was the only friend I needed.

When I was seventeen, I passed my driving test, and my dad treated me to a very used Toyota Corolla. It was love at first sight, despite the faded paint and scratched wheel covers. I immediately became a regular at the AutoZone store looking for mods and fun accessories. I'd spend most evenings out on the road, and it cost me a small fortune in gas. In my all-encompassing glee of auto-ownership and the freedom it gave me—and the fact my dad did an excellent job of hiding it—I failed to pay attention to his disappointment at being left home alone, and his failing health.

One night, I came home and found him passed out on the kitchen floor. His body was face down against the tile. The bowl of cereal he was eating was turned over, and the contents were strewn about the kitchen. The sight of him sent a shiver down my spine and for a few seconds I couldn't move. Then images of moments over the last few weeks played through my mind. Moments I must have seen but carelessly shelved as I ran out the door to go for a drive. When I really thought about it, my dad had been coughing more than usual, and I had on one occasion seen him take a couple of pills. At the time he seemed embarrassed like I had caught him in the act—a kid experimenting with drugs—but neither one of us wanted to dwell on it, so it wasn't explored further.

Our first visit to the hospital together followed. I could never get it straight in my head, which type of cancer he had. All I knew was, it was at "stage 4," and it had attacked several vital organs in his body. After his big secret was out, we both felt obligated to play our parts. He didn't want me at the hospital, and I couldn't stand to see him struggle. His family, who after hearing of his illness descended on us en masse, quietly enforced our cooperation with a look or a comment. They were so damn hopeful it drove me nuts, as anyone with half a brain knew he wasn't getting any better. The chemo treatments were destroying him.

Eventually, I was told he didn't have long. The information bounced right off my shield of not-wanting-to-acknowledge-horrible-things. The words "long," "didn't," and "have" were re-organized and confused into something easily forgotten. At the time I think I nodded my head and pretended to understand. I couldn't make eye contact with anyone, which they took as my heartbreaking, but surely, you'd have to feel one beating before that could happen.

Then "the day" came. Then another "the day" came. It was fucking unbearable. Dad's family hovered in and out of his hospital room and glared at me all the time. Some would encourage me to sit with him; others would give me dirty looks because I had stopped going into his room. After I heard "anytime now" from the doctor, I decided I didn't want to see the end. It was like, if I wasn't there then it never happened. The only important witness could not verify Mr. Pringate's last moment on Earth. Nope, didn't see it, you can't prove anything!

When I heard my dad call out my name, I ran away.

I could hear family call after me, a mixture of concern and outright rage. I think someone even chased me down the hospital corridor. They didn't even get close to catching me.

I smashed through the double doors at the end of the corridor and then took the stairs all the way down to the first floor. Once there, I kicked open the fire escape leading to the parking lot rather than risk a confrontation in the hospital lobby. I double-timed it to the far end of the structure where my car was parked and got in.

What was I doing? I pictured Dad reaching out for me, calling out my name as his bed, the room, and the entire family pulled away from me. He wasn't dead. He couldn't be dead. Right then, if I sat here in my car, everything would be fine. I was sure I would feel or see something if he had died. A sign. A flash of light. I would know.

The sound of his failing voice rattled around my head and wouldn't go away. Jesus Christ, what had I done? My thinking flipped, and I became my dad calling for his boy. I felt the energy leaving my body, and all I wanted was to hold his hand one more time. It was nice that the family is here, but I'd love to see my drive-thru buddy again.

I realized I'd made a huge mistake and got out of my car. I ran back into the hospital lobby and took the elevator up to my dad's floor. As I approached his room, my dad's sister walked up to me and slapped my face, hard. The rest of my family pulled her away. I was too late. They all hated me, I could see it in their eyes. There was no understanding, only incredible disappointment and disbelief.

Everything was muted. The doctor came out of my dad's room and opened his mouth. He started explaining things to me, his brow set to concerned. I didn't register anything he said as we walked into the room together.

He kept talking as I studied the lifeless body in the bed. It was calm, its face was relaxed, its arm hooked up to a machine. I felt we should be quiet for fear of waking him. The doctor squeezed my shoulder, still concerned, and then left me alone with the man in the bed. I studied his old face, his stubble, his bald head, his thick eyebrows, his pale skin.

My face was sore. Someone just hit me. There was something inside pulling me down, and my legs felt heavy. I tensed up and felt smaller. A bubbling inside rose from my belly up to my chest. My thinking flipped again, suddenly, violently, and I imagined the intense anguish of a dying man who wanted to see his son one last time, only to learn he'd run away.

My breathing became heavy. My heart pinballed inside my chest. My dad's lifeless body was in front of me. I was the worst person that ever walked the Earth.

V.

I put the photo in my pocket.

"Your dad seemed nice," says Christine.

"Yes, he was. He deserved better than me at the end."

"Do you think he would be proud of the man you became?"

What a horrible question. But I'm forced to think about it now and quickly conclude that my dad would not be proud of me. My lifelong call center job, the bad habits, the failed marriage.

"No, Christine, he wouldn't be. Thanks for that." I rub the back of my neck. "What I wouldn't give for a beer right now."

"There you go again with the beer. What would that solve?" asks Christine.

"Everything."

"That's weird."

"Is it though? There's nothing better when you want to tune the world out and take a break from your troubles."

I picture a tall Pilsner glass filled with golden lager, the slow rising bubbles, and the thick white head. I start to salivate. "You don't get it; you're probably too young. If you're stressed, in pain, even bored, a cold brew makes it all better. It's a great cure-all."

Christine looks confused. She probably doesn't meet many people like me in Heaven.

"Trust me. The world can be a shitty place, and life is nothing but one stressful event after another. If you find something that gives you a break from all that—beer, wine, meds—you stick with it."

"That sounds awful."

"Well, it feels more like freedom."

"But it's exactly the opposite of freedom. You mean to tell me you can't get through life without these things?"

"I guess not. But it's like that for a lot of adults." I feel a little shitty about this, but I'm done debating with the child, so I borrow a page out of Taylor's playbook. "Don't be so naïve. You'd understand this more if you'd lived longer on Earth."

That does the trick. At the mention of her death, Christine shuts the hell up.

That last comment about freedom sticks with me like a bloodthirsty tick. If I flip my thinking, then, okay, she might have a point. I'd needed a little help to get through the week. So what? Maybe it was a crutch, but I hadn't thought about it that way. As far as I'm concerned, beer clears away the anxiety and unlocks my potential.

Christine hands me Donna's little black phone book and then stomps out of the apartment. Inside, it's loaded with names and numbers. Donna knew a lot of people. Under "B" I find a single entry for Brad Hubbard. That's got to be the Brad asshole Donna was shacking up with. He's local too, and lives in the posh part of Anaheim Hills.

As it stands, I know Donna took out an insurance policy set to pay out $200,000. I just don't know how I was killed.

She had a motive, but I doubt she could pull off a murder. She'd more likely get someone else to do it for her and be in a public place with a friend when it happened. Maybe this Brad guy is as stupid as he looks. He appears to be a lot older than Donna and is probably thrilled to be dating someone young enough to be his daughter. *Creep.* He'd probably do anything she asks.

I stand up, fold the insurance paperwork, and stuff it into my pant pocket. My fingers touch the keys to the Plymouth, and I grab them.

"Come on," I say to Christine. "We're going to Brad's house."

"Brad?"

"My wife's boyfriend."

"What do you think you'll find at Brad's house?" asks Christine. My previous mention of her death is seemingly forgiven.

"I'm not sure exactly. My hunch is he helped Donna kill me. He may have even done the deed himself. In any case, we should probably keep moving. I have to know what happened to me."

We leave the apartment and head back over the road to the Plymouth. It's perfectly quiet outside, and I wonder when my hellish stalker, Eugene, will find me.

I open the driver's side door. Christine jumps in and climbs over to the passenger's side. I get behind the wheel and start the engine.

"This is kind of exciting, no?" asks Christine.

"What do you mean?"

"You, playing detective, looking for evidence, chasing up leads."

It is a little out of character, that's for sure.

It's a short drive to Brad's house in the hills. Since there's no traffic, I run the reds and before you know it, we pull into Brad's long driveway. *Rich asshole.* I would say he's totally Donna's type, but I find it hard to believe that he'd want kids. He had to be pushing sixty.

I get out of the car and Christine joins me.

"Wow, is this Brad's house?" asks Christine.

"I guess. This is the address Donna had for the guy."

The house is your typical multi-million-dollar home in California. It is probably at least a four-bedroom, two-bath place, with a separate office, a new kitchen, a pool, and . . .

"Hang on a second," I say. "I know this house."

Suddenly the image of two, magnificent, sexy as hell, boob-shaped Jell-O desserts enters my mind.

"Oh my god!"

"What? You've been here before?" asks Christine.

"You could say that."

I grab Christine's hand, and we head toward the front door. She asks questions about how I suddenly recognize this place, but I'm not in the mood to go into the details. I'm not about to revisit that point in my life again.

It is interesting how small the universe suddenly seems, or maybe just my part of it: a small life, limited connections, tiny world. I'm assuming, of course, the same lady I saw all those years ago still lives here. She could have moved on and my visiting would just be a coincidence.

The front door this time is unlocked—which my shoulder is grateful for—and it opens into a large foyer. To our left, there's the main living room, to our right, a dining and kitchen area. I walk into the living room, curious to know if the same people owned the house. It all seems so familiar. The furnishings look expensive, the artwork tasteful. They aren't billionaire-rich, but they are very comfortable.

On a shelf on the far side of the room I see some framed pictures, and lo and behold, there she is. Jell-O boob lady, with her Brad in a tasteful pose, professionally done. *The horny bastards.* I wonder how many men she had brought back to the house, and how many women Brad had on the side. I show the picture to Christine.

"Who is that?" she asks.

"I never got her name. Tell me, if a married couple cheats on each other but stay together, do they go to Hell?"

"It depends. If they cheated and kept cheating, then sure. Regardless of what was keeping them together."

"Really? Seems harsh."

"Well, they made a lifelong commitment to each other, George. If they keep breaking that promise they go straight to Hell. Sorry. The universe is forgiving, but there are limits."

I look at the picture again, and I feel bad for Miss Jell-O Boobs. She didn't know that all those years ago she was getting her ticket stamped. What if I was her last chance? Maybe the universe put us together to see what she would do. Did I do her a favor when I ran away? We were two ships passing in the night, being judged by some kind of universal energy, one for being unfaithful, the other, for not seizing the moment. I know Taylor said the universe wasn't like God as we knew him, but it still moved in mysterious ways.

"But she didn't break the rules," says Christine.

"What?"

"Samantha Hubbard. She didn't break the rules."

"How do you know that? You didn't even know her name a moment ago."

"I've got my connections, Mr. Pringate. And there's this."

I look to where Christine is pointing and see a medical degree mounted to the wall. I feel a wave of relief. Good for you Mrs., I mean, Dr. Hubbard, and suddenly the picture of that night gets a little clearer. There I was, twitching like an idiot, holding onto her magnificent boobs for dear life, and she was just probably trying to get back at her cheating husband. After I ran away like the coward I was, I bet she had a complete change of heart.

"But, she stayed with Brad?"

"She decided to stay and try and make it work."

"So, she's going to Heaven then?"

"She's already there."

"What? No."

"It's okay. Think about it. She was in her fifties when you met her. She died of old age and then went on to enjoy her afterlife."

I look at Samantha in the photo again. I'm glad she made it okay. Maybe, if I figure all this out, I'll see her again.

I put the photo back on the shelf and instruct Christine to search upstairs for anything that might connect me to Brad. I head to the kitchen and the fridge.

At first, I don't see anything, but then there, in the back, behind the family-sized tub of margarine, I see them—two bottles of golden Heaven. I check the rest of the fridge and am disappointed not to find more. Two bottles will have to do.

I grab them both and put them on the kitchen counter. In my haste, I try twisting off the cap with my bare hands, but these aren't the cheap domestic swill I'm used to dealing with. The sharp cap digs into my hand, and it hurts. I rummage around the drawers and cabinets looking for an opener, but failing that I can always use the countertop.

"Search is going well, I see," says Christine from the kitchen doorway.

"I thought you were upstairs."

"That was a stupid place to look, so I went to the office instead."

Christine steps forward and throws a notepad and some opened mail stamped "OVERDUE" onto the kitchen counter. They slide across and tap against the bottles. On the notepad, I see my address written down.

"You really can't control yourself, can you?" she asks, looking at the bottles. I suddenly find it very hard to look Christine in the eyes.

"Anyway, it looks like you were right about Brad. Without Dr. Hubbard's income, Brad was struggling to keep this house," says Christine.

So, there we have it, the last piece of this puzzle, and I'm so glad we're on a different topic. Donna had Brad twisted around her little pinky finger, and she got him to do me in. It makes complete sense to me. His dating pool had probably dried up and his chest pubes started to turn gray. He needed cash.

Then here comes Donna slinking into his life, and he's suddenly willing to do anything to make it work. I take a measure of solace in the understanding that Brad will end up in Hell, ideally via an arrest and lengthy stint in jail in the real world first. I am a little disappointed this murder mystery wasn't a little more complicated to solve, however. But perhaps human beings aren't all that complicated, and money has always been a powerful motivator.

"I'm going to wait outside for you to finish your beer," says Christine. She looks so disappointed I can't bear it. The way I see it, I have two choices now. Find a goddamned bottle opener and say "screw you" to the judgmental brat or go with her to answer one final morbid question about my death.

How did Brad do it?

I decide to do the latter, but I'm not happy about it. In fact, I'm super fucking pissed about it. I march out of the kitchen and outside. I'm all set to vent some frustration in Christine's face when I'm confronted with multiple new developments. First, Christine is driving the Plymouth— kneeling on the seat with her seatbelt on—and she pulls up right in front of the house. Second, I see a Chevy Express painted up to look like the GMC Vandura van from the television show *A-Team* barreling toward us.

"Get in, Mr. Pringate," says Christine.

"Is that supposed to be the A-Team van?"

"The what?"

I get in the car, and Christine somehow floors it. We peel out of the driveway and onto the street, the Chevy not far behind us. I look down at the pedals and see they haven't moved. "Wait, how are you—"

"Magic, Mr. Pringate. Just hold on."

With Christine driving Christine, we do surprisingly well against the faux A-Team van. After a couple of twists and turns, she heads down the way we came. The Plymouth proves to be a little too fast for the heavier van to follow. We get onto the 55 freeway and head north, then exit onto North Tustin Street. On the left I see the Denny's restaurant where this whole sordid affair began.

"Listen, Mr. Pringate. I'm going to leave you now."

"What? Why now?"

"It's time for someone else to take over."

Christine stops the car on the bridge over the Santa Ana River and gets out. I slide over to the driver's side, but stop short of putting the car in gear and driving away. Looking back at Christine, I see she is slowly walking, arms held out wide, toward the approaching van.

"What are you doing? You'll be killed," I say.

Christine keeps walking. "It's okay, Mr. Pringate. Eugene won't kill me."

"Are you crazy? He wouldn't think twice about running you down. Get back in the car."

Christine stops walking but doesn't turn around. "You've given me some stuff to think about, Mr. Pringate. Stuff I probably would've learned if I'd lived on Earth a little longer."

I have?

"Heaven isn't perfect. Some of the uglier parts of humanity don't make it there. It can leave a girl a little naïve about people and the world."

What on Earth is she going on about?

I can see Eugene now, behind the wheel. At first, his eyes are locked on me, but then they shift to Christine standing directly in front of his van.

It's like it all happens in slow motion. The van's brakes lock, and Eugene turns the wheel. Christine stands there, arms out wide. The van skids left and hits the wall at the side of the road. Taylor appears next to me, in the passenger seat.

"What the—"

"Time to go, Pringate," says Taylor.

"But Christine, she's—"

"Fine. Look."

I look back to the road. Christine is nowhere to be found. Eugene appears from behind the wrecked van, beaten and bloodied. But more than that, he's crying now. He falls to his knees, sobbing.

"What's up with him?" I ask.

"I told you Pringate; I'll do whatever it takes to save your soul. Christine is Eugene's daughter."

"What?"

"Eugene killed Christine in that car accident. He'd been taking something or other, washing it down with booze, before picking her up from school. Didn't even bother to check if she had her seatbelt on. She crashed right through the windshield. He took his own life soon after that."

I have to admit, I feel for the guy. "Seems harsh that you would use her like that. As a shield. To get to him."

"That's Hell, Pringate. This is what happens. No one will mourn Eugene's pain. No one will pick him up and talk to him, help him. That's what you're trying to avoid, Pringate. Now drive."

I turn around, close the driver's side door, and start to drive. In the rearview mirror, I can still see Eugene. Still on his knees. Still crying.

"I want to go home," I say.

"Not yet, Pringate. You have to meet your next counselor."

Chapter 4: Be Brave

I.

"So, you're telling me the universe likes strip clubs?"

"Let me put it this way: the universe doesn't hate them. It actually thinks they're a great challenge for humanity," says Taylor. "And don't give me that look. And don't get all judge-y about it either. Strip clubs are amazing places, George."

She doesn't elaborate, so I'm left to wonder what is so amazing about dank little buildings, hidden away on the outskirts of towns, filled with men suffering some kind of grand delusion. The women in these establishments don't like or love their customers, they might even hate them, yet the men somehow manage to convince themselves to the contrary. It's a fantasy built on lies with winners on both sides. The women get cash; the guys feel desired.

Stop kidding yourself, you've always wanted to visit one of these places. I have, haven't I. *That's probably why we're here.* More stimulation? *More stimulation.*

"Does everyone that goes to one of these places end up in Hell?" I ask.

"Not necessarily," says Taylor. "That's the amazing part. They are gray through and through."

"But if someone cheats on their wife with one of the dancers?"

"Well, if they have sex, maybe."

"And everything else is okay?"

"It depends what's in the guy's head at the time. If he's married and looking for someone else, then sure, he'll go to Hell if he's a repeat offender. Remember, the universe will give everyone a second chance. If he's the 'look and don't touch' type, then he's okay. Strip clubs are an excellent

107

sorting house, George. Sorting out the men who want to indulge in a little harmless fantasy, from the boys who have no self-control and can't keep their dick in their pants."

"But the guy upstairs can't approve, right?"

"Guy? Strange to think that God has a penis. That God has to take a leak sometimes. Ridiculous. The universe isn't a person, but a sentient energy that locked onto the human race's signal once you became evolved enough to broadcast one. You're not being judged by some bearded white dude sitting on a cloud wearing a robe, Pringate. You're being asked to judge yourself."

We exit the 91 freeway on North Kraemer Boulevard, then after a couple of left turns, we head down North Kraemer Place toward our destination, the Taboo Gentleman's Club. We park right in front of the establishment.

From the outside, it doesn't look like much, a simple white box of a building in an industrial zone. Big red lettering in stark contrast to the white walls says "TABOO" followed by slightly smaller lettering stating "Gentleman's Club." Then, just in case it still isn't clear what this place is all about, "Showgirls" flashes cursive pink neon. The building is located at the end of the road, which I find ironic.

"My third counselor is in there?" I say.

"Yes," says Taylor.

"Can't you just call him or her out?"

"No." Taylor smiles.

I sigh and climb out of the car. Taylor transfers herself over to the driver's seat. "Just go in there and take a seat. Your counselor will be with you shortly."

She puts the car in drive and leaves me at the side of the road.

I march up to the entrance and open the door. As expected, it's pretty quiet, with just a few men ogling the pretty—very pretty—women dancing for their amusement. The light coming in from the front door startles them, and they grumble in my general direction to either commit to entering their little world or not. Those directly caught by the light scurry back into the shadows like roaches.

I step inside and close the door. It has already crossed my mind that I might be able to get a beer here.

Once balls deep, as it were, I find a table at the far end of the club where the thumping music isn't so loud. It takes my eyes a few seconds to adjust to the room. Red is the predominant color. Red carpet, red curtain hiding the dancers backstage, red napkins, and red lighting. Whoever designed this place either liked to keep things simple, or simply didn't have a massive decorating budget. Everything else is painted black.

"Hi, I'm Candy," says a bubbly, bouncy girl. She looks to be around thirty-five, wearing what has to be a blonde hairpiece. She's not wearing much but compared to the other girls I've seen so far, she's practically formal in her crop top and shorts.

"Of course you are," I say slowly in a low crumbly voice, finishing off the scene from *Highlander*. I get a kick out of the exchange, but I doubt this Candy person knows what we just did.

Candy sits down next to me. She has an epic set of boobs under that crop top. Now I wish I had paid more attention when she first came over; I could have easily copped a look under her shirt as she stood over me. *Oh well, maybe later.*

"So, you're Georgie Pringate, huh?"

"And you are, what? My third—"

"—and final counselor, honey."

"Wonderful. And what are you going to show me? Pole dancing?" I gesture toward one of the dancers currently working said pole.

Candy laughs out loud, a little too loud. "You're funny!" And then more seriously, "Don't be like that."

"Like what?"

"One of those guys. Acting all dismissive, trying to be macho. By now you should realize that we know everything about you. And yes, I totally got what we were doing with the *Highlander* dialogue. I'm your last chance, Pringate. How does that make you feel?"

I look down at the table and sigh. If Candy is my last chance to make something of myself, to prove I'm worthy of Heaven or whatever it's called, then I think I'm screwed. I bury my head into my folded arms on the table.

"Not good, huh?" says Candy.

"So, what now then?"

"Drinks!"

Now you're fucking talking, and I bolt right back up ready for a drink. Candy gets the attention of a tall, burly dude working behind the bar—a black man, wearing a black T-shirt, jeans, boots, and a black leather waistcoat. He's enormous, and it's hard to tell where he ends and the club begins. He walks over and scowls at Candy.

"Hi there, ya walking, talking stack of shit," says Candy.

I watch for the big guy's reaction. He continues to scowl. *What in hell is she doing? Ask for a beer.* I know, but. *But nothing, ask for a beer!*

"I'm feeling a little playful at the moment and would like a cocktail. Do you think you could handle that? Not going to be too hard for you, is it?"

The big guy shakes his head slowly.

"Well, it's a miracle. The big lug can make a cocktail. Isn't that amazing, don't you think that's amazing, George?"

I look sheepishly up at the bartender as he turns toward me. "A-Am-Amazing," I manage to blurt out.

"Well then, shit stack, go make me an Orgasm, and my friend here will take a coke."

"I'll take a beer . . . And a shot, whatever whisky you have in the well is fine . . . Please?"

The bartender smiles at me as he walks back to his bar. Somehow, I don't think I'm getting that beer order.

"You should know better than that, Pringate."

"Oh come on, just one beer to take the edge off. You know, I've been through a lot recently, the least of which was dying!"

"Not a chance. You're an alcoholic."

It's not the first time I've been called an alcoholic. I've learned to ignore the accusation. *They're just being judgmental.* That's right, I've got this under control. *I have my routine.*

"I am not an alcoholic."

"Yes, you are, Pringate," says Candy. She taps her head and points to mine. "Remember, we know everything." She places a hand on my forehead in an over-the-top soothsayer kind of way. "You're thinking, you're not an alcoholic. That you just like your beer and what's the harm in that. You can't be an alcoholic because you don't drink wine. That you have a routine, or any one of a hundred ways you've managed to justify drinking until you black out."

I grab Candy's hand and push it away.

She continues, "You tell yourself you have it under control, that you don't drink during the week. That you completed a—" Candy seems confused suddenly "Dry January?"

"Ha, see! If I was what you said I was, how could I get through an entire month without drinking?"

"Georgie, the fact it has a name tells you everything you need to know about that."

I struggle to think of a comeback, and then the bartender returns.

"Diet Coke for the gentleman, a Screaming Orgasm for the bitch," he says.

I look at my Diet Coke like something had died in it. Candy shoos the bartender away. "Don't go too far, dumb-ass, we might need more drinks."

She takes her straw and stirs her milky white beverage, then lifts it to her mouth. What follows reminds me of the fake orgasm scene from *When Harry Met Sally*. Candy repeatedly slaps her hands on the table and moans as she downs her drink. I'd like to say, "I'll have what she's having," but we've already established that I am to remain sober, which sucks!

"Hmm, yes, YES, that's the stuff right there." She puts the glass down and sits there, staring at me, seemingly completely aware of the white mustache she now has. She licks it off her face and smiles, then raises her hand to get the bartender's attention. "Hey, asshole, same again." She looks at my untouched Diet Coke. "Just the Orgasm this time, dipshit."

"Why are you such a dick to that guy?"

"Oh, Dwayne? He's my boyfriend."

"You always talk to your boyfriend like that?"

"Well, I'm hoping to get into a fight."

Say what now? "A fight? Why?"

"To see what you'll do."

II.

After my father passed away, a good number of my family wouldn't talk to me anymore, being that the last time he actually needed me I was hiding in the hospital parking garage. They couldn't wrap their heads around the betrayal. Why I couldn't be there at the end.

This suited me just fine.

I didn't have to deal with them even when they were deciding who got what of my dad's possessions. I stayed well clear of that stress, and it wasn't like there was a lot of stuff worth fighting for anyway. I loved my dad, but he was shit with money. It turns out when you're having a great time eating out, going to the movies, and buying your son a car, there isn't a lot left to save. Dad pretty much operated paycheck to paycheck.

Once the family took their little pieces of him away, I had my car, the home theater system, and our collection of movies. The house sold quickly, and the measly amount of cash I got out of the deal mostly went to cover Dad's funeral expenses, medical bills, and credit card debt. In the end, I didn't have a lot of options.

One of my uncles begrudgingly offered to take me in, but that meant a move all the way to Ohio, of all places. That didn't sound good at all, so I opted to stay in California. A guy who worked at the funeral place, Scott, had overheard my family talking about me. He was looking to move out of his parents place too and wondered if I wanted to team up with him. I said yes and thanked my lucky stars. I had just turned eighteen.

We found a two-bedroom apartment near downtown Fullerton, California. It was certainly no palace, but we made it our own. A clash of pop-culture references competed for dominance as our individual tastes in movies and music collided. Scott's more colorful, Jamaican-inspired interests didn't always blend well with my passion for mainstream big summer blockbusters, cars, and synth-pop. Our bedrooms became ground zero for our respective tastes, and then the rest of the apartment was a collage of Scott's artful throws, beads, and incense, and my Depeche Mode, Voice of the Beehive, and Duran Duran posters.

Scott was an interesting guy. Tall with almost ivory white skin, and skinny, yet he carried himself like a much heavier man. He had a relaxed way about him and a wisdom beyond his years. Nothing much bothered him, yet he gave me the impression he could get quite serious if I stopped doing my share of the chores around the apartment. He had a quiet authority I wasn't about to test. It was an interesting time, and Scott was the closest I'd ever gotten to having a real living and breathing friend that wasn't my dad.

It was great, for a while.

To make ends meet, I waited tables at an Irish-themed restaurant called, The Muddy Farmer. I say themed because there wasn't anything remotely Irish about the place. It was essentially an American sports bar, painted green, and adorned with a few pieces of Irish paraphernalia. They served Guinness and corned beef and cabbage, but the TVs always played basketball, baseball, and football played with the hands, not feet. The most requested beer was domestic, and I'd forgotten how many burgers and pizzas I'd slapped down in front of happy, overfed customers during my time there.

The Muddy Farmer also introduced me to beer.

You see, the bullying at school, followed by my mother abandoning us and eventually my father's death, had left an unaddressed need in me. I was waiting for a solution to a problem I didn't know I had. It never occurred to me that there was any other way for me to be. I was George Pringate, and I was shy and awkward around people. I kept to myself and didn't even develop a rapport with any of our regular customers. Life's experiences had sculpted me into a meat sack prone to bouts of anxiety, and I didn't see any issue with that.

One night after a difficult Paddy's day shift, my boss— who claimed Irish ancestry via some unconfirmed connection to St. Patrick himself—served me my first beer. Just a regular old domestic lager, but by god it was wonderful. It was cool, crisp, and it tickled my tongue.

My boss watched me closely, and I felt a bit like a laboratory experiment. He had no idea what a revelation this was for me, how this simple liquid had opened a door, and that I gleefully skipped through it.

The "closing beer" then became a regular thing, a free drink after my shift before sending me home. As I settled in, one drink became two, and two became three. I took on more late shifts until I was closing the bar up nearly every night of the week. Once the manager trusted me more, he would spend more time in his office, giving me the opportunity for a swift one during my shift. Good times.

It was like I became myself, if that made sense. Like the real me was waiting for those beers to properly wake up and be an active part of the human race. I was more confident, happy, even better at playing pool. I got to know some of our regulars and even started using their first names. I was the man I always wanted to be after a couple of drinks, but only while the buzz lasted.

After a while, I wanted more; I'd beg my boss to sell me some domestic from our stock at the bar. At first, he was reluctant, being that it was illegal and all that, but relented when I agreed to buy the less popular stuff and at full bar prices. The crap beer he purchased on a whim from his sales guy who had promised him it was "the latest trend." It didn't taste very good but got the job done. As long as I agreed not to blab about where I'd got it, we had a deal until I'd cleared him out of the stuff. A neat, yet depressingly temporary arrangement.

While I enjoyed this setup, I needed to plan for what to do next. The thought of an interrupted flow of beer scared me a little. And by this point, I was still a couple of years away from being able to walk into the grocery store and buy whatever I wanted.

Hanging outside a liquor store and convincing someone to buy the beer for me was one option. There was also a chance I could find a less-than-ethical liquor store owner who would sell me what I needed. But California was strict about underage drinking, and I doubted I would find a sympathetic soul in Orange County.

It also crossed my mind that I could steal what I needed from the store, but I dismissed that right away. I knew myself, and no matter how I played the scenario in my mind, it always ended up with me getting arrested, then losing my job, then becoming homeless. Not good, and as it turned out, completely unnecessary.

My roommate Scott was a little older than me and had recently turned twenty-one years old. Fortuitous timing as my current supply of bland, crappy piss water I was paying too much for, was starting to run low. I figured I would ask Scott nicely, perhaps offer him booze for his trouble. Problem solved.

Not so much, it turned out. Scott didn't drink. Not only didn't he drink, but he was also actually opposed to drinking on some bullshit religious level.

So, I had to think about this. What would get goody-two-shoes Scott to willingly go into a liquor store and buy me the beer I needed? I could threaten to stop driving him to work, but that felt like a shitty thing to do. I needed a way to get him into the store without totally compromising his sensibilities, and he needed a way to justify this to his Lord and Savior. The answer came to me after my closing night libations, when I did my best thinking. I needed a higher power, a person with some authority over Scott.

I would have Scott's boss at the funeral parlor make Scott get what I needed. To do that, all I had to do was get Scott's boss into a conversation about his business, and from there, navigate my way around to the topic of booze.

I knew he liked to keep a stock of wine available, so I would start this conversation when I knew he was low on supplies. Luckily for me, he mostly bought reds and kept them in an easy-to-access location within the viewing room. Going into the viewing room might have been seen as a little odd, but if I played it as a nostalgic thing, I might be able to pull this off.

It was lucky I had my stash of beer from the bar to tide me over. It was murder watching my supplies dwindle as I patiently waited to put my plan in action.

I had already visited the funeral parlor once and saw they had four bottles left. A week later, I did another of my nostalgia calls and noticed they were down to half a bottle. I got onto the topic of booze—by way of some grieving parents who had lost their son. Did I feel guilty? Yes, but then a new voice in my head told me, *stay focused, we're all about the beer*.

I proposed that Scott and I go to the store and pick up wine for the funeral. Scott at that moment knew what I was doing, but I didn't care because his boss, busy with upset parents, happily accepted our help.

So, off we went. I made Scott help me load up with as many eighteen packs of Bud Light as I thought I could get into my car, enough to last me a couple of months, and then we purchased the wine separately. He complained, but what could he do? At least he could say he was forced into all this by his boss and thirsty roommate. His conscience, for the most part, would remain clear. His God, whoever that was, would still love him.

My plan worked perfectly.

Later that night, after my shift at the bar, I was ready to unwind and break open the first of my boxes. I sat in the living room with Scott, first beer in hand and a big smile on my face, when someone pounded on the front door. Scott got up to investigate.

I heard Scott say, "Oh shit!" Then he ran into his bedroom, and then back to me with a package. He handed it to me as he dragged me to my feet. "Take this into your room and lock the door."

From the feel of it, it was either a pillow-sized bag full of oregano or something you used to get cooked.

"What the hell?" I said.

"Just go!"

He pushed me into my bedroom, and I closed and locked the door. I reinforced it with my bedside dresser as I had a feeling the people at the door weren't here to sell or buy but to take.

As best as I could make out, there were two guys, and I heard raised voices talking about how Scott hadn't paid on time. It was hard to be sure because I couldn't hear clearly, but ultimately it didn't matter. Scott was in trouble with the wrong kind of people, and they were here to pick up the package which was now in my room.

The voices got louder and louder. It sounded like furniture around the apartment was being rearranged. Then nothing.

Someone pounded on my door, and I jumped back.

"Hey, come out man!" said one of the men.

I didn't say anything.

"We know you're in there. Open the fucking door!"

My heart was pounding, but there was no way in hell I was going to open the door. I backed away when it sounded like the guy was trying to break in again.

Through the door I heard, "Get that mother-fucker," followed by silence, and then maybe the sound of Scott getting dragged to my door.

"Tell him," said the guy.

Scott's voice followed. "Listen, George, open the door. I need that package I gave you."

I couldn't do it. I couldn't make myself open the door. I was petrified and I didn't want to get hurt. Even if I opened the door just enough to slide the package through, they would jump me for sure, and then probably help themselves to my beer. It wasn't like I could hide it all. I had so much I had even fashioned a chair of the boxes in one corner of my room.

"You coming out?"

As best I could figure it, if the slamming sound followed by groaning was any indication, Scott got punched in the gut.

"You coming out?"

There was more slamming and groaning.

"Jesus Christ, George, open the fucking door!" shouted Scott.

"Yeah, George, you coming out?"

I don't think I was breathing at this point. I could hear Scott groan and fall to the floor. I knew I should help him, let those assholes have the drugs, but I couldn't bring myself to unlock the door.

Police sirens could be heard getting closer, and the first thing that went through my mind was how this might be a problem for me. If they came up to this apartment, they'd find Scott all beat up, and it wouldn't be long before they found out why.

I heard the two guys bolt.

I pulled my dresser away from my door and opened it to find Scott was already up. He was closing the door behind the two guys that tried to rob him.

"The neighbors must have called the police. Help me get this place straightened up."

I didn't question why, I just hopped to it. I expected to find our place completely trashed, but in fact, only the dining room table had been tipped over, and they had broken one of Scott's lava lamps. It took less than a minute to fix and cover up.

I stopped to ask Scott a question, but he put his hand up to stop me.

"If the police knock on the door, you answer," he said.

I nodded. It made sense; he looked like he had done a few rounds with Mike Tyson. He walked around the apartment, turning all the lights off before heading for his bedroom. It suddenly was like nothing had ever happened. I stood silently in the darkness. I could hear my heart beating in my chest.

The sirens got closer and then stopped.

Flashes of blue and red light outside our apartment lit up our place like the world's cheapest disco. A knock on the door followed, and I answered.

Two police officers stood there. Both similar in height, weight, and hair color. It was like looking at clones. I got their names from the badges pinned to their chests. Smith and Jones.

Smith spoke first. "We got a call about a disturbance. Everything okay?"

"Yes, officer," I said back, trying my best to sound like a properly functioning member of society that couldn't possibly do anything like build a throne out of beer I shouldn't have.

Jones gave me a dirty look.

"Really? Your neighbor called and said she heard loud noises," said Smith.

"No, everything's fine, officer. I was just about to go to bed, but thank you for checking."

The cops exchanged a glance, then shrugged. "Okay then, sir. Goodnight."

"Goodnight, officers."

I closed the door, and a wave of relief washed over me. I walked over to Scott's bedroom door and knocked.

"Scott. The cops are gone."

Suddenly the door opened and Scott was in my face. He was pissed. "What the fuck was that, George?"

I couldn't respond, and my mouth opened and closed a couple of times like a dumb goldfish.

"I said you could give them my package," he said as he gingerly dabbed a tissue against his lip.

"I'm sorry, okay? I got scared." I walked back to my bedroom and returned with his stash. "And another thing. You wouldn't buy me beer, but this is okay?" Scott took the package away from me.

"Dude, I'm a Rastafarian!"

Then he slammed the door shut like that explained everything, and the conversation was over.

III.

"How long did you live with Scott?" asks Candy.

"I was out of there within a month."

Dwayne arrives with Candy's Orgasm, but instead of putting it in front of her, he tips the contents of the glass over her head. "Yeah, bitch, what are you going to do now?" He stands back and slaps his broad chest with his hands, daring her to do something.

Candy smiles. She lets a few drops of her drink land on her tongue as it runs down her face. "You ready, Pringate?"

"Ready? Ready for what?"

She stands up, a wry grin on her face, similar to the one Dwayne is now sporting. Is this a fight, or are they going to start making out? She removes her wig, revealing her short, dirty blonde hair underneath, and throws it at Dwayne as she charges at him. The wet hair slaps him in the face, and he's distracted long enough for Candy's wannabe football tackle, which barely moves the colossus an inch. With her arms around his waist, she keeps trying to push and lift, but it's pretty clear that Dwayne isn't going anywhere. I am suddenly distracted by the angle I have on the action. I can see right up her top!

Candy pulls back one of her arms and rams it between Dwayne's legs. This wipes the smile off Dwayne's face, but that's all it does.

He leans over and wraps his big arms around her waist, and then heaves her across the room. She lands on and destroys a table. The commotion causes people at the bar to take notice, but only briefly. This must be a fairly common occurrence in the Taboo, and they all go back to their drinks.

Candy gets up and runs back over to Dwayne and tries to punch him in the face. She doesn't even get close. He catches her fist in his big hand, and grabbing her by the throat, lifts her off the ground and throws her. Another table breaks her fall.

Neither of them are smiling now, and I've got the feeling they aren't playing anymore. Candy is hopelessly, ridiculously, outmatched, but she shows no sign that she is ready to give up.

Dwayne marches over to Candy and grabs her hair. She tries to take a couple of swings at him, but it is pointless. Her short arms can't reach him. He lets her try anyway, before smashing his fist into her gut. The force of the hit lifts her off the floor. Down she goes, doubled over in pain, struggling to breathe.

A few of the customers are now more interested in the fight than the naked dancer on stage. There is a collective "ooooh," as Dwayne lands his killer blow. A few of them look at me as if to say, "Are you just going to sit there?"

For my part, I'm not sure. I shift nervously in my seat, not knowing if I should get involved. What could I do against this giant anyway?

Dwayne reaches down and once again grabs Candy by the hair. Man, oh man, what is he going to do now? She is well and truly beaten. The crowd by the dance floor groans and moans, saying things like, "She's had enough Dwayne," and "Come on, man," and they continue to look at me, shrugging and making gestures like I should jump in and get involved somehow.

I want to, which surprises me. *Don't get involved*. But she's half his size. *Fuck that, she started it!*

Dwayne raises his fist again, ready to bash Candy in the face. What on Earth do they see in each other? I glance over at the dance floor. The customers have gone quiet, and some are looking away, preferring not to see what happens next. I look back at Candy, nervously pawing at Dwayne's fist.

I leap.

He brings his fist down.

Everything goes black.

When I come to, I find I am lying on the sidewalk outside the Taboo club. I'm not sure how much time has passed, but it's notably darker outside now. The first people I see are Dwayne and Candy.

"There's my hero," says Candy.

I rub my jaw. It hurts.

"Sorry about that, man," says Dwayne. "You jumped right into my fist."

They help me get to my feet. I'm a little unsteady, but once I'm up, I push away their hands and put a little distance between us. "You fuckers are crazy!"

"It was just a little role-play, George," says Dwayne.

"You were beating the shit out of her."

Candy moves in closer to Dwayne and hugs his big bicep. "Great performance, huh?"

"What?"

"He punches me in the gut, but I jump just a little before the punch lands. He throws me over a balsa wood prop table," says Candy. "We're stunt actors, Georgie. That is how we ended up in Heaven, after all."

"You're stunt people? So all that inside the Taboo was fake?"

What was I saying? Everything for miles around us was technically fake.

"Yeah," says Candy. "In our last job, I was a stunt double for Ronda Rousey, and this beautiful big lug doubled for Terry Crews. We had our date with eternity while filming a cheesy as fuck action film out in the desert. Our car blew a tire and sent us spinning. What can you do? Cheap ass film, cheap ass props."

"And they canceled production afterward. Our final moment never made it into theaters," says Dwayne.

"Yeah, but at least we checked out together, babe."

"That's right. No place I'd rather be."

They turn to face each other.

"We just staged a little area of the club to do our little experiment," says Candy.

"Experiment?" So, this is what it feels like to be a lab rat. Humiliating.

"Yes," says Dwayne. "And you passed, sort of." He pulls Candy in closer and she wraps her arms around his neck. A very passionate and difficult to watch kiss follows. When they finally decide to come up for air, Dwayne says, "I'll get the car. You sure you don't want me to go with you?"

"No thanks, babe. It's not allowed. Three counselors, remember?"

"What's going on?" I ask.

Dwayne disappears around the side of the building.

"You tell me, Pringate. Where to?" asks Candy.

"Well, I want to go to my apartment."

"Okay, then that's what we'll do."

A Ford Gran Torino, in red with a white Nike-esque swoosh, appears from behind the building and skids to a halt in front of us. Dwayne gets out of the car, the motor still purring. "I gotta say, Pringate, your taste in vehicles is tip top."

He gestures for me to get behind the wheel. I'm hesitant to go anywhere near him. He seems to understand this and backs away to give me some room. Candy lets herself into the car on the passenger's side. "Come on Georgie, let's go."

I slip by Dwayne and get into the car and close the door. Dwayne walks around to the passenger's side and gives Candy another overly long kiss goodbye.

It's okay this time though, because I've got my hands on one of my all-time favorite cars. I loved watching re-runs of Starsky and Hutch. With its crazy white stripe and 351 Cleveland V8, the car was the star of the show as far as I was concerned. By modern standards, it wasn't all that powerful with only 250 horsepower, but with this car, it was all about the presence.

"Are you just going to fondle the controls, Georgie? Let's go to your apartment," says Candy.

"Right," I say as I shift the car into drive, imagining I'm David Starsky going out on another investigation.

After we're back on the road, I ask Candy a question. "Back there, when Dwayne said I sort of passed your test."

"Yeah?"

"What did he mean?"

"Well, we were wondering if you'd get involved. Do the right thing."

"And I did, right? I mean, that's what this is about? Why am I still here?"

"You got in the way, Pringate, that's all. You jumped—" Candy laughs as she tells the story, "—headfirst into his fist." She does a little reenactment, pushing her head forward and then snapping it back while simultaneously crossing her eyes and sticking her tongue out to simulate the punch that knocked me out.

"Har. Har."

"It's not nothing, Pringate. You put yourself in harm's way for me. But we'd be more convinced if you had lasted a little longer, or got involved sooner. Maybe a little one-two with the big man."

"With that guy? You're out of your mind."

"Yeah. You still would have gotten your ass handed to you, but we'd be more convinced that you'd learned a little something about living."

"Getting into fights is living?"

"No, trying to save me might have been."

"But it was all fake."

"You didn't know that at the time."

I drive out onto La Palma Avenue. "So, jumping into your boyfriend's fist is living?"

Candy sighs the sigh of an impatient teacher getting tired of her dim student. "Not completely, but it's one aspect of life. Getting into a fight for the right reasons counts, going on a vacation to a foreign country counts, getting promoted at work counts. Doing something creative and trying to share it with the world counts. There's plenty of ways to do it, but you have to do it. Be a nurse, a cop, fight fires, join the foreign legion, or help the needy. You've been holding yourself back, and until you start being honest with yourself, you're going to fall through the cracks."

I think back to the scripts at home sitting on my desk. "I write."

"Yeah, and who has read your work, Pringate?"

For that, I have no answer.

"Exactly, so what good are they?"

We continue in silence for a while. I had always meant to show people my work but, was too afraid of what they'd say. Donna sneaked a look at one of my scripts while I was sleeping once. I remember she woke me up to tell me how much she had enjoyed it, that I should contact an agent, but I never did.

I turn left into my apartment complex and park in front of the main office.

"We're here," I say.

Candy looks out of the window and doesn't seem impressed. "I expect we get a lot of clients from this apartment complex. It looks like the kind of beige palace where souls go to stagnate."

We get out of the car and Candy goes to the trunk. As the trunk lid slams back down again, I see that she has a shotgun.

My apartment is located in the building directly ahead on the second floor. When we get up onto my balcony, I notice my door has been left open. Candy immediately steps in front of me and with a finger to her mouth, she signals for me to be quiet.

Could Eugene already be here? It was stupid of me to suggest coming here. I'm not even sure what I expected to find. All I know is that Brad had my address written down, that's it.

She whispers, "I'm going to go in there. You stay here. If you hear gunshots, you run or get involved, up to you. Okay?"

I nod and stand at the top of the stairs, ready to run.

Candy enters my apartment in full S.W.A.T. mode, carefully checking every angle before moving further in like she's done this before. My place is not very big, so she's in and out in about thirty seconds, turning on lights on as she goes. As she reemerges, she looks ashen. Eugene isn't in the apartment, but something is, and it has shaken the unshakable Candy.

"What?" I whisper.

"I don't think you want to go in there, George."

"Why, what did you see?"

She speaks past me, as though I'm not here. "I knew Taylor was . . . But I didn't think she'd . . ." Candy turns to me. "I think we should go. Eugene could be here any second now," she says.

I push past her and enter my apartment. Everything is as I last remember it; my sofa, my dining room table, the stack of dishes in my sink. There doesn't seem to be anything untoward going on, no murderous agents of Hell lurking in the shadows. Candy hasn't followed me in.

I go into my bedroom and find my unmade bed and my desk, laptop, and extra monitor, all as I left them. My most recent script notes are taped to the wall. Everything seems perfectly normal.

To my left is my sink and I walk over to splash some water over my face and neck. In the corner of my eye, I spy something in my bathtub.

I fight my mind. I know what I saw. *Someone is in the tub.* You know who that is. *No, it can't be.* Sure, it can. *But we had this mystery all figured out.*

Suddenly it seems my body is made of clay and it is so hard to move. I reach for the doorway leading to the bathroom. I take a deep breath and turn on the light inside.

There I am, in the bathtub, in my pajama shorts and a black T-shirt—the real me, with my potbelly, skinny arms and legs, sitting in a pool of my own blood.

Quite dead.

Just as I had planned.

IV.

As things were going south with Donna, I started to think about suicide. It was funny how the thought of ending one's life suddenly became "a thing." One day it wasn't there, and it never crossed your mind, the next it was a new morbid option on the table.

At first, I quickly dismissed the idea, but as the weeks and months came and went, I thought about it more and more. It started out as an interesting exercise, in a way.

These thoughts were usually more intense the second day after one of my Friday night binges. You'd think they'd occur during the worst part of the hangover, but no, it was the day after, when the headaches arrived in the mail.

Hangovers for me didn't go like they're shown on TV. I didn't get horrible headaches right away, and I wasn't sensitive to loud noises or bright lights or anything like that. I just felt run down, and my stomach would need a big breakfast before it felt stable again. I also had very little enthusiasm for, well, everything. I preferred to drink ice-cold energy drinks and fester on my sofa.

This was another thing that frustrated Donna, and she soon tuned into this little routine and went about her day without any contribution from me.

Day two of the hangover saw me mostly recovered. I'd be in the mood to get things done, in between sudden and intense headaches, followed by severe bouts of depression. During these fits, it seemed like my world was coming to an end. I'd sit at my desk, head in my hands peering through my fingers at items around me. They'd looked like props, like I was eavesdropping on my own life. When the emotions I was feeling got too much, I'd burst into tears. This often helped, but the thoughts of suicide would enter and linger in my mind.

I'd wondered how I would do it. A bullet, an overdose, jumping off an overpass onto the freeway. Initially, these were just thought exercises, a morbid "what if." I would play a scenario out in my mind and see where it took me. A bullet through my brain would probably be the quickest way to go. I'd have to save up and buy a gun and do a little training on how to use it. Then maybe find an isolated spot, someplace with a beautiful view to do the deed.

I did worry about getting it wrong, however. Maybe as I pulled the trigger, I'd have the gun at a weird angle and only blow my face off or something. Then I wouldn't get what I wanted, and everyone would know what I had tried to do and be on high alert. I'd likely end up in a clinic for suicidal losers, sitting in circles talking about feelings through my fucked-up face.

The overdose and bridge ideas I dispensed with almost immediately. Taking a bunch of pills just sounded like it would force me to vomit, and jumping off a bridge wasn't guaranteed and I might hurt someone else in the process.

Whatever route I took, it had to be mostly painless, affordable, and not hurt anyone else.

I started to think about finding an artery to cut. I could take a scalpel to my wrists, make a long cut up my arm to be sure I got the job done. Or, even better, I could find that big old vein in the upper part of the leg. I'd seen John Lithgow in an episode of Dexter cut open someone's thigh. That would almost certainly rule out the possibility that I'd be saved, should someone run in on me while I played surgeon on myself.

That was what got me thinking about the bathtub too. Mr. Lithgow had put his victim in the tub before making his incision. I could fill the tub with nice warm water, climb in, end myself, and any mess to clean up would be confined.

My thoughts would then turn to how to get my affairs in order before I went to the sweet bye and bye. I would want to be found after death, and before my body started to smell. If Donna did leave me, this would mean directly contacting the emergency services. With no real friends, or even fake social media ones to speak of, what else could I do?

It would all come down to the timing.

I'd set up a text message to 911, and then hit send as I felt myself slip away. I might underestimate how I would feel or how quickly I would go, but I would try nonetheless. If no text got sent, it wasn't like I was going to care.

I'd clean my apartment from top to bottom and make sure everything was spotless. Then I would close my various accounts: bank, utilities, Netflix, Amazon, etcetera. It did cross my mind that various government agencies would look for activity like this and send someone to check in on me. But then I thought, that would prove big brother existed, and they'd hardly blow that cover for a call center employee that felt sad. I would eliminate all cookies and website history, however, just to be safe, and leave my computer's password, and the contact number of the closest member of my family.

I'd make my last wishes very clear in my letter. I wanted to present an organized life with very little baggage to process. I wouldn't want to put anyone out too much or have overdue notices arrive in my mailbox after I was in the ground—a nice clean getaway.

As my plans started to take shape, things got a lot more serious for me. Could I do this? Could I drag a sharp blade across my inner thigh and bleed out? It would only be a second of pain before I began to fade away. The detail in my plans started to make this all feel possible, and then one night I might have told Donna in a fit of beers and tears. To her credit, she probably tried to talk to me about it, but the next morning I had no concrete memories of what I said or did, and she wasn't talking to me.

After Donna left me, I started to spend some time in the tub, and I purchased a scalpel. I'd mock cut myself and then pretend to go limp. I'd close my eyes and stop breathing for a moment as I pondered what would happen next. Would it be like falling asleep? Would I see a tunnel of light? Maybe

I'd end up being a social worker in Hell like in the movie *Beetlejuice*.

I decided I should have a pillow to rest my head on. I would also like to be dressed in my pajama shorts and a T-shirt. That way I wouldn't have to cut through fabric, but still be covered up when the paramedics arrived. I did this night after night, my sad little performance, even during my Friday binge sessions.

Scalpel at the ready.

V.

I wasn't murdered. I did this to myself.

I sit on the floor and rest my head on the toilet lid. I've never felt so damn sorry for myself, and I start to cry big ugly tears. I feel like I may never stop crying and I'm okay with that; a lifetime of hurt is pouring out of me. This was my life—one sorry, sad excuse of a life—sitting dead in a bathtub. There I am with my face partially buried in a pillow. My mouth open and my eyes shut. My skin is almost as white as the bathtub, in stark contrast to blood-red water.

Why did I come here? I should have taken Brad's note with my address on it to be proof enough that I was murdered. I could have quite happily finished this ridiculous game never knowing what I had done to myself.

"Hey there," says Candy. She pokes her head around the door. "How are you doing?"

"Go away."

I don't want to play this game anymore, and I don't deserve Heaven. It is time to give up.

"I'm just going to wait here for Eugene. Okay?"

Candy leans her shotgun against the cabinets outside, somehow manages to slide into the tiny bathroom, and takes a seat on the edge of the bathtub, blocking my view of the late George Pringate.

She takes my head into both hands and uses her thumbs to wipe away the tears running down my face. "George, what did you do?" She breaks off some toilet paper from the roll beside my head and cleans me up a little. I try to pull myself together.

I look directly into Candy's eyes. She's softer than before, a look of genuine concern on her face. I take solace in that.

"I killed myself."

"Why?"

I sit up and rest my head against the wall. Over Candy's shoulder, I can see myself again. "I had been planning it for months. Night after night, sat there in the tub, daring myself to do it."

Fresh tears fall down my face.

"This is what I wanted."

"I know, honey." She breaks off some more toilet paper and hands it to me.

"I couldn't see a way forward. I was getting a divorce, and I had no savings. I'm in my forties, Candy, and I still work in a call center making fifteen bucks an hour for Christ's sake. The walls were closing in on me, every avenue was . . . I had nowhere to turn. Do you know how that feels? One by one the doors were closing. Then you realize you're the one closing them. In the end, I couldn't do it anymore, and I wanted out."

A horrible realization comes over me. I look at the cheap linoleum floor, as though the broken jigsaw pieces of my life were there, ready to be assembled. The image of my lifeless body in my mind, demanding me to take a cold, hard look at my life and make the connection I had always pushed away. In my heart of hearts, I knew why I was here.

"George, I need you to do something for me."

I look back up at Candy.

"Do one brave thing, right now. I think you're ready," she says.

"What?"

"One brave thing, George, now."

One brave thing? The answer comes to me quickly, somehow. What had been a constant through all of this? *Don't do it you fucking asshole, don't spoil this.* The one thing pretending to lift me up, but which ultimately dragged me into a bathtub. *Look, you're feeling down, I know a cure for that.* Waking up on Saturdays, beer cans strewn around my apartment. *So what? You were having fun.* The hangovers that lasted two days. *It was worth it.* The judgmental stares from people at the grocery store. *They were jealous of your freedom.* The rumors and snide comments at the office. *Fuck them!* This had to stop; I had to give myself a chance.

"I'm an alcoholic."

"There you go."

Suddenly, we were both startled by a loud bang in the living room. Candy leaps up, grabs her shotgun, and then helps me to my feet. She leads the way and pokes her head around the door. "Huh? That's unusual."

She signals to me that it's okay.

I walk into the living room to find Brad standing there, a befuddled look on his face. A revolver in his hand. "Brad?"

He slowly scans the room, his eyes wide open, unsteady on his feet. I step forward and take him by the shoulders to steady him. "Brad. What are you doing here?" Then I notice a small hole in his temple, leaking blood. The bullet that caused it left a matching hole on the other side of his head. I shake him, and he finally looks me in the eye.

"George? But . . . You're alive?"

"No, actually."

"Then . . . Then what's going on, George?"

"I'm not entirely sure." I look to Candy for answers, but she just shrugs.

"What do you remember?"

"I remember . . . I came here to . . . But you were already . . ." He gives the revolver a confused look. "But that can't be right. You're here."

"And in the bathtub too."

"Yeah, that's right. You killed yourself, George. Why did you do that?" Then he seems to remember something that makes him angry. "And then that bitch wife of yours killed me!"

I let go of Brad's shoulders. "What?"

Brad begins pacing up and down the room. "We'll go and kill George, she says, make it look like a suicide, she says. Collect the insurance money and take off to Mexico, she says. After it's done, she says, 'Sorry, Brad, the insurance pays out quick if it's a murder.'" Brad looks at the gun in his hand, and I realize how stupid it was not to take it off him right away. "Then she takes this gun out of her bag, presses it up against my head and bang, I'm here with you."

"I guess she wanted to make it look like you killed yourself too," I say.

"Yeah, except that doesn't make much sense, does it? Who am I to you? And why risk presenting a mystery to the police? Donna had a recording of you—you were drunk again, crying about wanting to kill yourself, describing how you'd do it. If she stuck to the plan, all she'd have to do is show that to the police, and we'd be home free."

Oh jeez, she recorded me. I remember her trying to talk to me about it, but I don't recall her using her phone. I bet she played the concerned wife perfectly.

"Well, she clearly couldn't wait for the payout," says Candy.

Brad throws the gun onto my sofa and gingerly touches his wound. "But why am I . . .? What is this . . .?"

"You are here to help me, Brad." Taylor walks into the apartment and closes the door.

"Who the hell are you?"

"Well, I'm not your Transition Consultant that's for sure. Your fate has already been decided."

"My fate?"

"Yes. You are guilty of multiple accounts of adultery, and you planned to kill George," she gestures her hand like a game show assistant toward me, "so you are going straight to Hell." The same hand then points a thumb downward.

"Hell? There IS a Hell? Oh, come on? So I slept around a little. George wanted to die. Donna made me do it."

"Twelve women, Brad. Twelve," says an unimpressed Taylor.

"And I didn't kill George."

"That's true, but intent still counts."

"And what about Donna? What happens to her?"

"Don't worry about her. Donna's ticket is well and truly stamped. In fact, word from the living tells me she's likely going to spend the rest of her days in a jail cell. At least three people in the apartment complex saw her leave after they heard the gunshot. She is not the brightest bulb."

"Well I tell you one thing, I'm not going to Hell for that cow." Brad makes a run for the door. As he opens it, his head explodes. Taylor, Candy, and I all jump back as pieces of brain and skull smash against the wall. A familiar voice calls out as Brad's headless body falls onto the patio.

"Hey, George. Miss me?" says Eugene.

I can't see where he is, but judging by the location of the little pieces of Brad's brain slowly running down the wall, I'm guessing he was standing on a second-floor patio adjacent to us.

"Hey Taylor, you in there? Dick move using my daughter like that on the bridge. You must be fucking desperate."

"Needs must when the devil drives," shouts Taylor.

"Fuck you! Come out, George. Let's end this nonsense. End the argument, okay?"

Candy turns to Taylor. "What was Brad doing here?"

"I just borrowed him, a little detour on his way to Hell. I figured Eugene would take care of it, and he did," says Taylor. She turns to me. "I told you, Pringate, I'm willing to bend the rules on this one." She snaps her fingers and the front door slams shut. "You've made some progress, George. Now let's see how much you want this."

Great. More ambiguous crap from my Transition Consultant.

With another snap of her fingers, she's gone in a flash of blue electric light.

Chapter 5: The Finale

I.

After the first big hole appears in the front door, Candy and I duck back inside my kitchen at the other end of my apartment. More shots ring out, and more holes appear in my walls—bits of plasterboard fly over the kitchen counter and land on our backs. I very much doubt the kitchen cabinets will save us if Eugene directs buckshot in our direction.

From outside, I can hear Eugene laughing. "You still alive, Pringate? Who's with you?"

Candy slides around the entrance to the kitchen and up to the front door. She takes a shot at Eugene through the hole he created. "It's Candy, asshole, and you're not having him." She lets off another shot before joining me again in the kitchen.

"Candy?" Then it's like he suddenly remembers who she is. "Oh, Candy! Hey, that boyfriend of yours isn't with you, is he?"

"Why? You worried about getting an ass-kicking?" she shouts back.

Eugene responds by making a few more holes in my apartment. The air fills with smoke and dust and smells of burned wood as buckshot tears through studs and wiring in the walls.

"Well, Georgie. Get us out of this," demands Candy.

"Right," I say. "Sure, no problem."

My apartment complex is a series of large buildings, and each building has sixteen apartments arranged onto two floors. Each floor is made up of two rows of four apartments. I have a corner unit, which means I have a neighbor below me, one to the side, and one behind me. We've never met.

"I have an idea."

I grab a steak knife out of my sink and, keeping low, I make my way back into my bedroom. Candy follows me.

To the right of the bathroom sink, I have a small closet. Seeing all the holes being punched through the walls reminds me of how flimsy these apartment complexes are, and I decide our best bet is to cut through the plasterboard into the next apartment. I clear my clothes out of the way and get to work. The apartment we are heading for must be the same floorplan, only mirrored, so I expect to emerge into my neighbor's closet.

Eugene continues, at a somewhat leisurely pace, to take shots at us. Windows shatter, debris flies everywhere. Most of his shots seem to be deliberately aimed high like he isn't in any rush to kill us and wants to see how much damage he can do first.

"Nice plan, Georgie, but if I understand this correctly, Eugene will have a clear shot at us when we try to leave by your neighbor's patio, right?"

I stab into the wall and saw downward. "Once we're in, we'll have more walls between Prince Douchebag and us, and we can cut another hole from the other living room into the living room of the next apartment over. Once we're in that second living room, we'll have a way out that Eugene can't see." I stab the wall again, about twelve inches to the left of the original cut, and start sawing. "Could you maybe keep Eugene occupied? I'll come to get you when I'm done."

"Aw, my hero." Candy crabs her shotgun and heads for my living room. I soon hear her aggressive response to Eugene's attempts to kill us.

I make the first hole on my side of the wall and then cut another on the other side. My hands begin to tire, and I need to shake them in between cuts. Once my second hole is finished, I squeeze past the studs and push past an extensive collection of ladies' shoes stored inside cheap-looking space organizers. After that, I run into the living room and start working on the hole that will lead to another living room, and then outside.

A little more muffled now, the gunplay between Heaven and Hell continues in the background.

I get less fussy about the kind of hole I make and pull at the plasterboard once I have cut enough away with my knife. With my side now clear, I decide to kick the plasterboard leading into the next apartment.

The gunplay stops.

I run back to the closet and find Candy struggling to crawl through the hole in the wall. She hands me her shotgun, and I help her get past the shoes. It looks like she has been grazed by buckshot, and blood runs down her arm.

Eugene calls out, "Candy. You okay, hon?" Though he doesn't sound all that concerned.

"We've got to go," says Candy. "It's not going to take that asshole long before he figures out we're gone."

Eugene calls out again, "Caaannnddyyy?"

I help Candy to her feet. We head into the living room and then through the hole I made into the apartment next door. From there, we make our way outside and downstairs.

"Where to now, Georgie?" asks Candy.

We hurry away from the apartments while I think of what to do next. We can hear Eugene calling out our names and blasting my apartment. Going back to our car doesn't seem like a good option since it is too close to Eugene's position. We'd have to continue on foot out of the complex and then maybe get another vehicle. Candy's arm looks terrible, and I notice we have left a trail of blood behind us. I tear off the sleeve of my shirt and wrap it around her arm.

"There, that should help," I say.

"You got a plan?" asks Candy.

"Working on it. Let's get out of this complex first."

As we approach the outside edge of the complex, I see the top of the Wholesome Choice supermarket over the perimeter wall. The store had recently closed and might be a good place to hide.

To hide? There I go again. Not this time. Fuck that. No. Way. Flip the thinking, Pringate. My thoughts should be less about getting away from Eugene, and more about taking him on. I've had enough of his shit, and this ex-supermarket looks as good a place as any for a grand finale.

"I've got an idea," I tell Candy.

She follows me to the gate, and onto Chrisden Street. I want to put a bit of distance between us and Eugene, so I start running.

"Oh boy, you had to start running, didn't you," says Candy.

I turn to see her trying to run after me with her good arm holding down her crop top to maintain coverage. Her heels scrape against the concrete. Her shoes are ridiculous, set on a two-inch-tall platform at the front, with easily a six-inch-tall heel, and the whole thing is festooned with crystal embellishments. How had I missed these before? Oh yeah, that's right, I was staring at my dead self in a bathtub.

"Take your shoes off."

"You did not just tell me to take off my six-thousand-dollar Christian Louboutin's."

I have no idea who this Christian fellow is, other than possibly a con man, but his shoes were going to get me sent straight to Hell. I suspect I will be able to thank him personally if that comes to pass.

"Take them off, now!"

Candy grumbles, but complies. Once I have the shoes, we start running.

I try a few of the entrances marked "staff only" located along the side of the building, but they are locked. So we head through a passage further down before making our way to the front of the store.

I cup my hands around my eyes and stare through the glass doors. Inside it's a big space with rows and rows of empty shelves. Lots of places to hide and maybe even plan an ambush.

The doors, predictably, are locked, but one good swing with one of Candy's boots takes care of the glass, and we are inside. Candy puts her silly shoes back on, and then we make our way to the end of the aisle directly in front of the doors to keep an eye out for Eugene. This also puts us near the entrance to the warehouse, which means we can keep an eye on that too in case Eugene comes at us from that direction.

"So, what's the plan, George?"

"To tell you the truth, I'm not sure."

"Well, you had better come up with something soon. It's not going to take Eugene long to figure out what happened to us."

I begin to formulate something in my head, a way to distract Eugene long enough to get the drop on him, but I need more help if I'm going to pull it off.

I turn to Candy. "Can Corporal Green join us?"

Right then, the Bandit Trans Am smashes through the entrance into the supermarket. It skids to a halt right by the cash registers. Out pops Corporal Green, wearing his trusty Stetson and a very broad smile.

Green calls out, "You rang, partner?"

Candy and I walk back to the front of the store. I immediately go for the guns I know will be on his back seat.

"I'm here too, Mr. Pringate." Christine carefully steps over the broken glass door.

"What? Who is this?" asks Green.

"I'm Christine. Mr. Pringate's counselor."

"Well isn't that adorable. Pringate, you brought a kindergartner to a gunfight."

"I never—" Then, seeing Christine again reminds me of the bridge. Eugene crashed his van in order to not harm his daughter. Maybe Taylor thinks we could use that to our advantage. "She's fine."

I grab a shotgun and a box of shells. I throw another box of shells at Candy, which she catches and follows with a quick, "Thank you, kind sir."

Corporal Green helps himself to the two pistols I had so carelessly discarded in the desert after our first meeting. As the belt goes on, he smiles. "Just like The King in the movie *Charro!*"

I roll my eyes at his Elvis reference and walk over to a panel of switches on the wall by the main entrance. I flip them all on, and the fluorescent lights blink to life around the store.

"Okay everybody," I say to my gang of afterlife counselors.

Christine raises her hand.

"Yes, Christine."

"Can I get a gun?"

"No, Christine." She drops her hand, folds her arms and starts to pout.

"Why the lights, Georgie?" asks Candy.

"Simple. I want to make sure Eugene finds us."

My three counselors exchange looks, but don't say anything.

"Now, this way." I walk back into the store, and my team follows me.

"What's the plan, Pringate?" asks Green.

"I'm planning an ambush, Corporal Green."

"Sounds promising."

II.

I am an alcoholic.

I am an alcoholic.

I am an alcoholic.

As I tell myself this over and over again, I'm filled with hope.

I thought that if I ever did finally admit to being one, it would be like acknowledging I was a terribly flawed person. A "recovering alcoholic" is what I would have to tell people, and you were never allowed to say you actually recovered, job done. "Why, certainly I'll have that drink because I am now fully recovered, thank you very much."

No, you were a "recovering alcoholic" for all eternity.

I had met people who used this term, and it was all they ever talked about. They'd wait until you offered them a drink and then let you have it. "No thanks, I'm a recovering alcoholic." You'd then apologize like you'd even be able to tell, and they'd immediately start talking about their experience in all its gruesome detail. They all had their "rock bottom" story—a tragic tale that led them to their moment of clarity.

It was important for them to tell their stories—more for themselves than for anyone else—but I feared the arguments still raged inside them. They'd go to AA meetings to make friends, and find support in that community, but they were all still fighting to stay one step ahead of their demons. It honestly sounded exhausting. Their faith in God played a part in their recovery. But what if you didn't believe in burning bushes and commandments? Was there an Alcoholics Anonymous for atheists?

If only my dad had talked to me about my mother and why she left. If only the teachers at school had stopped the bullying. If only my father's family had the wisdom to know I was just a frightened teenager, unable to deal with my dad's last moments, I might have turned out okay.

That's wasn't it. I flipped my thinking again. Why didn't I try to talk to my dad about Mom leaving? Why didn't I fight back at least once against the bullies at school? And how hard would it have been to spend time with my dad as he passed away?

I was damaged goods waiting to find my preferred poison. Once I did, it was the only thing that ever stopped the argument inside my head and kept my demons at bay. It wouldn't last, of course, and required more and more beer to keep the voices happy, but it was the only solution I had, and now that I was being honest with myself about it, the only one I cared about. I was quite happy to crawl inside a twenty-five ounce can of beer and spend the rest of my life there.

I killed myself. Years of trying to self-medicate my problems away finally did me in. A life not lived; was there going to be any other conclusion to it? My own deadly "rock bottom" story.

I rejected that this was my destiny to end up dead in a bathtub, however. This wasn't fate, this wasn't an act of God—I caused it to happen. Tom Hanks would just be some guy called Tom Hanks if the movie industry hadn't come calling. He'd be working a nine-to-five, or maybe picking up people's trash. Just a regular, everyday person, with a wife and a couple of kids, probably struggling to make ends meet like the rest of us. No one would ever say, "I really thought old Tom would become a Hollywood legend. Oh well, that's life I guess."

He had a talent that he cultivated into a successful career. All the great actors and musicians and artists did. The fame, awards, and fortune didn't find them; they had to go out and get them. Lives lived well.

I put myself in that bathtub; I was the one in charge.

Maybe I was being a little hard on myself. It wasn't like there weren't mitigating circumstances. But destiny is just a word, and not something you should hand the keys to. A little honesty, a little self-reflection, could have changed my life. Therapy, medical science, the tools were there, but I let the alcohol rewire my brain and lock in the pain I was feeling. It turned me into an introvert, scared of the world.

I am an alcoholic.

One step. Recognize what tempts you and take a step back, even if you don't want to.

Focus. Give yourself a moment and don't let the racing thoughts overwhelm you.

Be brave. Push forward with your life and take some risks.

I thank the universe and my counselors for second chances. For the first time, I see a way forward—a tiny light at the end of a long tunnel. It's a lifeline, and I grab it and hold on tight. I need to make the most of this opportunity and make it work for me. I screwed up my life on Earth, but maybe I could make something of my afterlife. Acknowledging my problems with alcohol was just the beginning, and there is more work to do.

III.

The Wholesome Choice seems bigger than I remember. That's probably due to how empty the place is. The last time

I was here, I hadn't known about the store's closure and walked in to find picked-over shelves and worse still, no alcohol.

With the lights on and the Trans Am parked inside the entrance of the store, I have no doubt Eugene will find us, but the wait is unbearable. I have Candy covering the front door, and Corporal Green is patrolling the warehouse. Christine has stayed with me.

"Do you know why Taylor picked you to be my second counselor?" I ask Christine.

"Because of my dad?" She looks down at her shoes. "She probably figured I could shield you."

"How do you feel about that?"

"At first I thought it made sense."

"And now?"

"After meeting and getting to know you, it seems a little cruel. For my dad, I mean."

"And for you too, don't you think?"

It is always hard to look at Christine's adorable young face and remember she is actually a teenager. Having died at such a young age, growing up in Heaven must have at first seemed like a dream. A forever Peter Pan–like experience, oblivious to the ugliness of the real world.

"You don't blame the accident that killed you on your dad anymore, do you?"

"It's more complicated now."

"Because you know he had a problem with drugs and alcohol?"

She nods.

I think I have discovered a flaw with Heaven. Growing up there means Christine wasn't exposed to the uglier aspects of life on Earth. On meeting me, Christine's thinking about her father got a little more nuanced, a little grayer. For the first time, she maybe saw her father as a victim that needed support, and not a hellish villain to be judged.

"You think you could forgive him?"

Before she can answer, the pop of gunfire erupts near the front of the store. Corporal Green emerges from the warehouse. I take Christine's hand, and we keep low as we make our way down the last row of shelves at the far end of the store, away from the action.

Reaching the end of the aisle, I squat down and risk a peek. Christine gets down on her hands and knees and crawls around me to take a look.

"Hey," I say, pushing her back behind me. "Stay back; it isn't safe."

"Mr. Pringate, I can't die here. I can help."

She did have a point. "I realize that, but I need to do this myself. Besides, I'm sure the universe wouldn't like me hiding behind a little girl."

The gunplay stops, and I can see Candy's Christian Louboutin boots sticking out from behind the Bandit Trans Am. She has been taken off the board.

Eugene appears and stands over Candy, looking smug. He's dressed in black again and holding an injured arm. Candy must have clipped him before she died. If I make it through this, I'll be sure to thank her for the help. I picture her back in the enormous arms of her boyfriend, Dwayne. It would be nice if she could tag him into this game. I'm sure he'd want to talk to Eugene with his fists right about now.

Eugene opens the passenger door to the Trans Am. He probably saw Corporal Green's gun collection and decided to help himself. His head disappears from view.

Just as I'm starting to wonder what happened to Green, a blast from his shotgun smashes into the driver's door. I can't see clearly, but I think Eugene jumped into the car at the last second. I need to get closer. Turning to Christine again, I say, "Stay here, okay? I'm not kidding." I get no complaints this time.

I jump and slide across the space between the aisle and last checkout, then squat behind the registers as I get closer to the action. From this angle, I can see the back of the Trans Am.

The Trans Am engine roars to life, its wheels spinning on the smooth waxed floor. Shotgun ready, I keep myself low and walk behind the remaining registers toward the car. Green gets in another shot and hits the windshield. At that range, he must have hit Eugene, but the car lurches forward and starts doing donuts inside the store. It runs over Candy's body and knocks Corporal Green on his ass. It isn't lost on me how useless my afterlife squad has been at taking on Eugene, but now that I think about it, maybe that was their plan all along.

The piercing sound of the squealing tires is unbearable. As the car spins toward me, I can see Eugene steering the car with his left knee while he uses his hands to load a gun. I let him have it. Click click, BANG, click click, BANG. My shots are wild and off-target as I struggle with the recoil, but I do manage to hit a side mirror and the passenger's side door.

Green gets to his feet. "That's it Pringate, get him! Whoo-hoo!"

I'm scared, excited, and I jump rapidly to every emotional level in between. Am I taking charge of my life? It feels like I am. My heart thumps inside my chest, but I'm not going to run away this time. This asshole isn't going to stop my recovery. I keep firing and take out the rear brake light and the truck lock. The lid pops open revealing more target-practice fruit. My next shot hits a watermelon, which explodes, sending melon pieces everywhere.

As the front of the car swings around for a third time, Eugene has what looks like an automatic rifle poking out of the hole in the windshield. I duck and take cover behind a cash register as he begins to fire. Bullets blast through the register and a hole appears right above my head. The air reeks of burnt wood as I crawl back the way I came, moving clockwise and contrary to Eugene's spinning Trans Am.

Corporal Green is not so lucky. I get back to the end of the register and onto my feet, just in time to see Green take multiple shots to the chest. I was right; my squad was deliberately being sucky at this protection lark. Green doesn't even have his weapon up. His last actions are to give Eugene the finger and shout, "Wanker!"
This was my fight to lose.

Before the car spins around again, I take off and run in front of the registers until I get to the aisle where I left Christine. But she isn't there. Frantic, I look around, but there is no sign of her. Shit!

The Trans Am stops spinning. Eugene struggles to get out of the car. He looks bloodied, tired, but determined as ever. I duck behind the shelves, but the heel of my shoe bangs against the metal base of the shelving unit. Eugene looks right at me, smiles, and sends a fresh round of bullets right at me.

Sparks fly as bullets rip through the metal shelves. I uselessly cover my head as I sprint down the aisle. It's a wonder I'm still in this game. My only hope is to get to the warehouse where I can hide and maybe get the drop on that asshole. It's at least a hundred meters to the entrance, however, and he has to know it's my only option too. This is going to be close.

I run toward the warehouse. I don't look around for Eugene. I almost make it.

BANG. My knee explodes, and I can't imagine how anything on Earth could be more painful. I crash to the ground and drop my gun; my lower left leg is barely hanging on. It seems like there's only a couple of pieces of unbroken skin holding my leg together.

Everything is in slow motion, and I slip in and out of consciousness. Each time I open my eyes, the looming figure of Eugene, my afterlife Terminator, jumps closer.

No, this can't be the end. I will not allow it. By sheer force of will, I stay conscious. I locate my shotgun and start to crawl toward it.

But Eugene is standing over me now.

"Pringate, you asshole!" he shouts. "Time to end this stupid contest because I'm tired of getting shot." He giggles like you do when you're exhausted.

I look him straight in the eyes. "Fuck you! I want to live my afterlife!"

"Mr. Pringate, catch!" shouts Christine. She grabs my shotgun and slides it across the floor into my waiting hand. Without delay, I lift it up and fire and hit Eugene in the belly. He isn't even looking at me; he's staring at Christine. The blast knocks him off his feet.

Christine runs over to me, and on seeing my leg, says, "Ew, that's gross!"

Eugene groans and rolls over onto his side, and then he manages to push himself back against a shelf. Tears run down his face.

I get Christine's attention and whisper in her ear. "Knowing what you know now, do you think you can forgive him?"

Christine's eyes well up, and she hugs me. "I don't know."

Looking over her shoulder, I fix on Eugene's bloodshot eyes. There's a longing there; he looks so damn vulnerable.

"Go on, Christine. Go to your dad. Help him," I say.

I suspect she wants this too, badly. There is so much pain shared between the two of them. All it needs is a little understanding and a forgiving heart. She doesn't waste any more time. She sprints over to Eugene, arms wide. "Daddy!"

Eugene drops his gun as he takes Christine into his arms.

He immediately starts to look better. His skin clears up and gets some color, and his hair grows back too. It's not long before the hole in his belly starts to heal, and he's able to get onto his knees to meet Christine at eye level.

They briefly separate a little so he can hold her head in his hands and kiss her forehead. They start to laugh together as Eugene looks at his arms and hands, and touches his face.

He looks over at me. "This was your idea, Pringate?"

"I think it was Taylor's."

"But I borrowed a page from your playbook, Pringate," says Taylor, as she emerges from the warehouse. "A higher power."

That's right. Eugene's higher power was his own daughter. I try to sit up, but fail.

"What are you still doing on the floor, Pringate?" asks Taylor.

"My leg, it's—" I look down at my leg and find it's perfectly fine. "Oh, cool." I get up and stand next to Taylor. There's an odd energy around us and a sense that things are coming to an end. I look toward the front of the store. The Trans Am is gone, and the front doors are whole again. My afterlife counselors, Candy and Green, are gone too. Then beyond the front doors outside, the white fog returns. It pushes up to the building and then pours through the spaces around the edges of the door. The thick fog spreads outward, hiding everything it touches.

My thoughts turn inward. I think I did everything I was supposed to do. It was, however, never explicitly spelled out to me, so there's some doubt.

"So, what happens now?" I ask.

"What happens now, Pringate," says Eugene, his tone suddenly more serious, "is that you're still coming with me."

He winks at Taylor, then lifts his gun and fires.

I feel the tiniest amount of pressure in my forehead and then, nothing.

IV.

I wake up. I am in my bed, in my apartment. My clock on the nightstand says it's 8:23 a.m.

Did I make it?

I check my stomach, chest, and arms, and I am happy to discover I am still in the more-perfect-me body. I am wearing my trusty pajama shorts and a black T-shirt.

Getting out of bed, everything feels mostly normal, and I take needing to pee as a positive that internal bodily functions are operating within normal parameters. I make my way over to the bathroom, though slowly. The last time I saw this room it had my dead body in it.

No rotting corpse this time, phew. Just the usual levels of soap scum and dust, so I step inside and relieve my bladder of its contents.

That's annoying; I'm out of toilet paper. I'll get some at the store today, no problem.

After peeing, I use the sink to run some water over my hands. I dry them and then walk into my kitchen. While I figure out my afterlife status, I may as well make coffee.

Damn it, I'm out of filters; I could have sworn I had some. Oh well, I'll add that to the shopping list. I wonder what day it is so I check my phone, but the battery is dead. God dammit. I plug it into the charger and after about a minute, the batteries have enough juice to start my phone's operating system and I find out it's Saturday.

Okay, I'll get dressed and go to the store. I'm sure Taylor or one of the other counselors will be along to explain things shortly.

On the way back to my bedroom I stub my big right toe on the doorframe. Shit that hurts and I look down to see that I bent the nail. A thick white line forms along the entire width of the nail about a third of the way down. I'm reminded of my first meeting with Taylor. No toilet paper, no filters, no charge on my phone, fucked up toe. No, it can't be. Can it?

Then I recall the smiling face of Eugene holding a gun aimed at me right before the lights went out. Did he win? Did I get sent straight to Hell? And after we reunited him with his daughter. Ungrateful bastard.

I need to find Taylor and figure the best place to look for her would be the Denny's where all of this started. Twenty-two minutes later I'm showered and ready to go. I add toothpaste to my shopping list.

Outside it's like any other Saturday morning in my apartment complex. People I don't recognize are talking dogs for walks and doing their laundry. Nothing especially hellish about any of it. And my car is where I remember leaving it in my carport.

I get into R2. I say "Good morning, R2," as is the custom, and we take off down Chrisden Street. At least my car seems to be working.

I break down on the Lakeview Avenue 91 freeway overpass, or more accurately, I run out of fuel.

Damn it, this isn't fair. How could I possibly be in Hell? I got involved in the action. I was instrumental in getting Eugene and Christine back together. I had come to an understanding about my alcoholism.

Cars honk at me as I sit in my dead car. So, this is Hell. I've only been here half an hour, and I'm already miserable. What will I be like after a day, or a week, or a month? I'll probably end up back in my bathtub.

A black Porsche pulls up behind me. A woman gets out, and I immediately recognize her. It's Miss. Jell-O Boobs.

She is wearing a pretty yellow summer dress, a much softer image than when we last met. She looks to be around my age.

I lock my doors as she approaches, which feels kind of stupid, but I'm really not sure about anything, and I just want to feel safe. She knocks on my window once, and then again when I don't respond. "Come on, George, don't pull this shit with me again."

I wind down my window and say, "Hi."

"What are you doing?" she asks.

"Nothing. My car, it's out of gas."

"Oh, well, you want a ride to the nearest gas station?"

I am immediately suspicious. "You'll have to excuse me, Jell-O Boobs, but I'm new here. What's going to happen at the gas station. Do I get robbed? Does it explode? I think I'll wait out eternity right here, thank you very much."

"Did you just call me Jell-O Boobs?"

I sink into my seat and look away, embarrassed. "Sorry." As I nervously try to explain why I called her that, I fear I'm making it worse. "Because of that time . . . When you . . . You know?" I use my hands to gesture the act of grabbing her breasts, and I even grunt as I do it. So, so stupid. "We almost . . . Jell-O was all I could think about."

She bursts out laughing. A big beautiful laugh that makes me smile. "Oh my god. You poor thing. I wondered what was going on. If I did anything wrong."

"Oh no, you did nothing wrong." I unlock the car and get out. "You were just my first, anything, and I got nervous." I do a little shaky reenactment for her at the side of the road, and she laughs again. I could listen to that laugh forever, but I feel the need to ask, "So, you ended up here?"

"Here?"

"In Hell. I was told you went to Heaven."

She smiles. "Having a bad morning, are we?"

"You could say that."

"Don't worry, that's probably Taylor fucking with you. You made it, Pringate; this is Heaven."

I give her a sideways look. "Heaven is a broken down car on an overpass?"

"It all depends on who you're with, right?" She steps into my bubble, and I'm surprised I'm okay with that.

Looking into her beautiful emerald eyes, I say, with a clear, confident voice, "I guess it does."

We stare at each other for a moment and then she breaks the spell. "Come on. Let's go."

"Go? To get gas?"

"Or whatever."

She walks back to her car's passenger's side door. "Here, you drive." The keys are thrown at me and I catch them.

"Cool."

We jump into the car, and I start the engine. "Where to?"

"I think we should go to the park. Head up this road and turn left."

"What about my car? It's blocking traffic."

"Don't worry about it. It'll magically end up back at your apartment. I promise."

Leaving my car behind, we drive to Peralta Canyon Park and a wonderful surprise.

Pulling into the parking lot, I see all but one of the spaces are occupied by my favorite movie cars: the Trans Am from *Smokey and the Bandit*, the actual van from *The A-Team* television show, and the original Love Bug. The Bluesmobile is here, and the Gran Torino from *Starsky and Hutch*. It's like a car show for movie lovers. Even cars that were not used in my rehabilitation are here. The DeLorean from *Back to the Future*, the custom-built Mercury from *Cobra*. You name it, it's probably here.

I park in the one available space, and we get out.

Close to the parking lot where we parked, in and around two gazebos, a gathering had been organized. Samantha takes my hand and guides me toward the people, waiting for me.

It's all too overwhelming, and I grin from ear to ear. A big sign hanging between the two gazebos says, "Welcome to your afterlife, George Pringate," and I start to recognize the people clapping and cheering. Samantha lets go of my hand as I get ambushed by people. The police officers, Smith, Jones, and Cartwright. The seedy guys from the Taboo Gentleman's Club. Corporal Green, Candy. All dressed for a perfect summer picnic, though Green still has his Stetson on.

I hug everyone, shake hands, and even cry a little. In each gazebo, food had been arranged, a potluck lunch, cakes, sandwiches, soda of every kind. I don't spot any beer, however, and I'm upset when it disappoints me. I should have known I'd have more work to do, even here in the afterlife space. There are no magical solutions to alcoholism, no quick fixes. I imagine it'll get easier as time goes by, but for now, I'll have to keep a close watch on my demons and reach out for help when I need it.

Sherryl, the waitress from Denny's, walks past the gathered people with two boob-shaped Jell-O desserts on a plate. This gets a huge laugh and I hang my head down in embarrassment. I do, however, look up in time to see Samantha wink at me.

Corporal Green approaches me, with Elvis. The younger, pre–weight gain, beautiful Elvis. He shakes my hand and I'll admit, I'm a little star struck.

"Congratulations, George," says Elvis.

"Th-Thank you."

Green puffs his chest out and rests his thumbs inside his belt. "Now, George, I want you to apologize to The King here."

"Apologize, for what?"

Elvis looks confused and doesn't seem to know where this is going.

"For what you said about The King's acting."

Elvis closes his eyes and pinches the bridge of his nose. "Aw, come on now, Green. My acting sucked, and you know it."

I smile as the self-righteous look on Green's face changes to one of abject horror. "I know no such thing. You were an awesome actor."

As Green pleads his case, Elvis leads him away, and he gives me a nod as he consoles his number one fan.

"Mr. Pringate."

The crowd around me parts to let Christine through. I barely have enough time to squat down as she collides with me and gives me a big hug.

"It's so good to see you," I say.

"I'll say," said Eugene, who was standing a few feet behind her. God, he looked well. Clean shaven, a full head of hair, still wearing that awful pineapple print shirt, but still, full of life. Or should I say afterlife now? So much to learn.

"Sorry about shooting you and all," he says.

I separate myself from Christine and stand up to shake his hand. "No problem. You had me going there for a while."

The people around us chuckle at this.

Eugene looks me directly in the eyes and says, "Thank you, for everything. If you need any help, with, you know . . . Don't hesitate to call. Maybe we can help each other?"

"That sounds good. Thanks, I will," I say.

Taylor finally makes an appearance, carrying her big blue binder against her chest. "Right, everyone, go find something to eat. I have some paperwork to go over with George here."

The crowd disperses and surrounds the tables loaded with food. Taylor guides me to a table far enough away that we can have a private conversation. Once settled, she opens her binder. I keep my eye on the people getting their food. There's one person I haven't seen yet.

"So, George. You made it. Congratulations."

I turn back to Taylor. "It seems so. Thank you. For everything."

"No, thank you, you helped me reclaim one of my old clients."

It took me a second. "Eugene?"

Taylor nods. "Losing him was bad. It bothered me, so I was hoping someone like you would come along and help me fix this and educate Christine a little. My boss is very happy with me right now, I can tell you that."

Boss? "God?"

"If that's what you insist on calling it, fine."

"Is he coming here today? I'd love to meet him."

She seems entertained by this. "So would I, but I don't think it has a body."

"Oh. So, what happens now?" My gaze returns to the party.

Taylor finds the page she's looking for and pulls it out of its plastic sleeve. She hands it to me. "This is just a closing statement acknowledging and thanking everyone here for their help."

I see some legal-speak text and a list of names: Candy, Green, etcetera. I don't read it, and I take the offered pen and sign my name at the bottom.

I look over at the party again, a little disappointed. This day was almost perfect.

"What's wrong, George?"

"I was kind of hoping to see my dad." I hate to think it, but I have to ask. "I guess he didn't make it?"

"Of course he did. He looked after you, didn't he? Look again, George, he'll be here somewhere."

I look again. Amongst the sea of faces talking and laughing, there's one I recognize staring right at me. Looking as he did before his cancer diagnosis, which weirdly puts us at around the same age here. Dressed in his favorite dad jeans and a short-sleeved dress shirt, which is tucked in.

"Are we finished?" I ask Taylor.

"Yes. Go say hello to your dad."

I get up, and I don't know whether I want to run or walk. I end up doing something in between. He does the same. When we meet at first, it's a little awkward. We can't seem to settle on a handshake or a hug, but pretty soon we're in each other's arms.

I only want to do one thing. "I'm so sorry, Dad." I burst into tears. "I'm so sorry I wasn't there at the end."

"It's okay, son, I understood."

We separate, and he places his forehead against mine. He's crying too. We look the same age, but I still feel like the teenager he hung out with all those years ago. "It's okay. I was sorry to leave you. Sorry I didn't talk to you about your mother. Sorry I wasn't there to guide you."

"I didn't do a whole lot with my life."

"It's okay, son. This universe is all about second chances. And it looks like you're getting a handle on things. I hear you helped bring Eugene back."

We turn to look at Eugene sitting with his daughter. She hits his nose with some cake, and he retaliates with a tickle attack.

"She's still a kid?" I wonder.

"I expect that's to help Eugene settle in. She'll go back to being a teenager eventually."

My dad takes a hanky out of his pocket and wipes his eyes, and then hands it to me. I do the same.

"Now, listen. All is forgiven."

He puts his arm around my shoulders as we walk to the people gathered around the food.

"You're going to love it here. It's like Earth, but everything—politics, government, the social order—operates in optimum balance."

"How?"

"Because there are no greedy, evil assholes living here, that's why. This place represents the best of the human race, son. You can do whatever you want here. Be the best version of you."

"Sounds great. Do you want to go somewhere, catch up?"

"Maybe later, son." He winks at me. "I met someone here, and I have a prior engagement. But don't worry, we have the rest of eternity to catch up and go on new adventures together. You won't believe this, but I've gotten quite good at surfing."

We stop by the food. He looks down at the table and sees a plate of mini Jell-O boob desserts. "What's with the little boob desserts? Seems to be a theme with you for some reason?"

"It's an awkward story," I tell him.

I look around and catch Samantha standing by herself. She looks over at me, and our eyes meet.

"You know what, Dad, you're right. We'll catch up later. Okay?"

He turns away from the food and then follows my gaze to where Samantha is standing.

"Oh, right. Good luck."

As I walk over to Samantha, I feel the love of the universe coursing through me. Am I free of all my demons? No, but for the first time in my life, I think I have the tools and support to keep them under control, and maybe one day, I'll defeat them.

I want to hold on to this feeling and never let it go. I want to talk Samantha into going on adventures with me. I want my dad to teach me how to surf. I want to check out the cars in the parking lot. I want to see if anyone will read my scripts.

I want to live my afterlife well.

Acknowledgements

It really does take a village, and this book would not be possible if not for several important people. To my beta readers, John, Esther, Liza, and Jon, I thank you. To my editor, Cindy Jewkes, thank you for your patience, I know I can be a challenge! To my proofreader, Mark Schultz, thank you for making sure everything was ready to publish. And finally, to my critique group, Amanda, Alana, Brian, Craig and Dana. I thank you for your wisdom, and guidance as I put this story together.

About the Author

    Stewart Hoffman was born in Doncaster, England, and spent the first ten years of his life growing up in the nearby village of Rossington. After that there were several hops around the globe before he settled again in sunny Southern California. Stewart is a web developer, a world traveler, and a storyteller. He's also an avid reader and a film fanatic armed with his own blog.

More from Stewart Hoffman

The Bug Boys (book 1)
The Bug Boys vs. Professor Blake Blackhart (book 2)
The Bug Boys and The Bullet Ant Queen
(book 3 – coming sometime in 2020!)

Social Media

https://twitter.com/stewartfhoffman
https://facebook.com/stewartfhoffman

Website

http://www.TalkieGazette.com

36886791R00107

Made in the USA
Lexington, KY
18 April 2019